I0670615

Totally Bound Publishing books by Aurora Russell

Single Books
The Au Pair and the Beast

Anywhere and Always
Falling for the Tycoon
Snowbound with the Billionaire
Guarded by a Hero

Minne-sorta Falling in Love
Semper Fitz
Mac of All Trades

Minne-sorta Falling in Love

MAC OF ALL TRADES

AURORA RUSSELL

Mac of All Trades
ISBN # 978-1-80250-980-9
©Copyright Aurora Russell 2022
Cover Art by Kelly Martin ©Copyright September 2022
Interior text design by Claire Siemaszkiewicz
Totally Bound Publishing

MAC OF ALL TRADES

Dedication

First, this book is dedicated to my own grumpy ogre, who was extra supportive over the course of this book's journey, and to our two little mini-ogres, who fill every day with surprise and joy.

For my dad and stepmother, who have always believed in me… I'm thankful every single day for your love and support. For my brother and sister-in-law, for being awesome and always willing to answer obscure questions on a moment's notice.
For Minnesota, which will always hold a part of my heart.

Finally, this book is dedicated to all the brave men and women who risk their lives every day to protect us. You have my deepest respect and eternal gratitude.

Chapter One

"I have to admit that I'm impressed by how well you handled all the questions from the police about Brock Templeton," Lana said grudgingly. Joe 'Mac' MacKenzie was already much too cocky, and his ego hardly needed any stroking. Watching him with the officers, though, had been like watching a master. She could easily see how he'd earned so many promotions and honors as a Navy pilot.

He shrugged, not taking his hands off the wheel, but the small smile he gave — *and why couldn't he be a little less handsome?* — was self-satisfied. "It's the accent," he answered, really laying it on thick. "Like my daddy said, a Southern man tells the best jokes and is always welcome at any dinner table or gatherin'."

She snorted, and not the usual elegant sniff that sometimes escaped but a full-on nasal rattling noise. "You sound like Tom Hanks' cousin from the deeper South — like, the Mariana Trench of Alabama."

"Oh, no, ma'am, not Alabama — perish the thought! My family's pure Georgia. How did you guess I was from Mariana Trench, though?" he teased. "My granddaddy was mayor of Mariana Trench, as a matter of fact."

She raised one skeptical eyebrow. "Matter of fact, *eh*?"

Her heart felt like it beat double-time at Mac's charming grin, flashing like the Cheshire Cat's as it was lit periodically by the streetlights they passed. *Lana Fitzhugh, you of all people know better than to get your head turned by a handsome, charming man,* she scolded herself. He'd shown himself to be overbearing, jealous and possessive when he'd fired one of the caterers on the spot earlier in the evening without even consulting her. *But you didn't disagree with his decision,* the annoyingly honest voice in the back of her head forced her to acknowledge. The caterer had actually been making her uncomfortable, but it had been *her* problem to deal with, not Mac's.

"Would I lie to such a stunning creature? You wound me, ma'am, straight to the core." He pretended to be hit by a bolt to the heart, and she couldn't help the burble of laughter that she tried to stifle. He was just so ridiculous. He was smart, funny and seemed truly dedicated to helping other men and women who'd recently left the service. Several times over the past few weeks as she'd worked closely with him to plan that night's fundraiser, she'd found herself liking him in spite of her better judgment.

The party had been an unqualified success for the worthy veteran's charity that Mac and Fitz, her second-oldest brother, had become very involved with. *Well,* she mentally amended, *it was practically perfect until Brock Templeton, Fitz's fiancée's ex-boyfriend, made a scene, insulted Clara and drunkenly confessed to trying to cause her to 'accidentally' lose their baby.* Brock had clammed up when they'd gotten to the police station, but, thank goodness, Mac had already recorded everything on his phone.

"I know that Fitz and Clara will really appreciate your getting the police to agree to take their statements tomorrow. They don't like to leave baby Hope for too long," she answered, sobered by the recollection of the night's events.

"I'm certain they've checked in on Miss Hope, but I do believe they may be doing some, uh, private celebrating of their engagement, too—or, at least, on behalf of lonely single dudes everywhere, I *hope* they are. It's not every day that a man gets the woman he loves to agree to marry him." Mac's voice was light, but there was something sad behind his tone, just below the surface.

"No...no, it's not," she agreed, snapping her mouth shut when she realized she sounded wistful. She had plenty to be grateful for, especially now that Fitz had returned to their lives, bringing the lovely Clara and Hope, shaking up the household and breaking their oldest brother, Drew, and Lana herself out of the cold, boring routines they'd fallen into. "Clara is just lovely—and Hope, too. I couldn't be happier for them," she enthused, perhaps a bit too heartily.

Mac quirked one side of his mouth up in a wry smile. "You've convinced me...but are you sure you've convinced yourself?"

His insight surprised her.

"I suppose you're right...but please don't think it's about Clara, because she really is wonderful. I truly am happy for them." She paused, forcing herself to be truthful. "Maybe a little envious, too. A long time ago— *God*, when I was so young and arrogant, self-assured to the point of naiveté and convinced of my own completely irresistible self—I made some really awful decisions."

If he'd said anything, she probably wouldn't have continued, but he remained silent, waiting.

"I ended up with a badly trampled heart—let's call it pulverized instead of broken—and it cost me my best friend and years of my relationship with Fitz, too." Suddenly uncomfortable with just how much she'd revealed, she gave a weak laugh. "I'm sorry I said that...*burdened* you with that. You didn't ask for my life story."

Mac touched his hand to her thigh for an instant before returning it to make a hard turn with the steering wheel. "Whatever happened, it sounds like you learned a lot from it, although I'm sorry it sounds like it caused you so much pain," he replied in a low, earnest voice, so different from the light, teasing tones he usually used with her. "And, Lana, nothing you could ever tell me would be a burden," he finished, clearing his throat. She wondered if he was equally uncomfortable with what she'd revealed.

Taking pity on him, she deliberately lightened the tone. "I bet you say that to all the young debutantes," she answered. "Does it ever work?"

Mac's laughter was a surprised bark. "*Touché*, Miss Fitzhugh. It might shock you to learn that I have, indeed, known my fair share of debutantes, including my two sisters."

"Now, that *is* unexpected," she agreed, although now that she pictured it, she could definitely see Mac all dressed up in a gray afternoon suit, flirting shamelessly and fetching lemonade for some pretty young thing. "Does that mean you can dance? You never asked me once tonight."

They stopped at a signal so that his face was half in the light and half out, but the expression on the half she could see was distant. The silence between them became thick and uncomfortable. Lana knew she must have mis-stepped, but she wasn't certain how.

"I don't think I can dance anymore — or at least not like I used to," he answered at last, his voice gruff. "I lost my right leg below the knee about eighteen months ago now."

Lana sucked in a sharp breath. She'd known Mac and Fitz had met in a military hospital, and she'd noticed that Mac walked with a limp, but she'd never wanted to pry, figuring that Mac would tell her about his injury if he wanted her to know. She'd never imagined he'd lost part of his leg entirely.

"Horrified? Tempted to feel sorry for me?" Mac sounded defensive. "I've had to deal with just about every type of reaction."

She touched his shoulder gently. "Nope, just surprised, since I didn't know," she answered quietly. "I can't even begin to understand how difficult recovering from an injury like that would be, and I admire your charity work even more now."

The enclosed space of the small front seat of the car felt suddenly intimate, especially so late at night, as if the two of them might be the only people awake in the city — or maybe in the world.

They pulled onto the long driveway — well, really a small, private lane — that led to the main house of her family's compound — Fitzhugh's Folly, as it was widely known, given how outrageously expensive and ostentatious it had been when her grandfather, Pat, had built it.

Tonight, it looked cavernous and dark…forlorn. *Or maybe that's just me*, Lana thought, but recognizing the source of her melancholy didn't make her feel better. Her oldest brother, Drew, had opted to stay at his high-rise apartment downtown to save time before his morning meeting. Her grandfather and Roger, who was ostensibly their butler but really a member of the family, along with being her grandfather's long-time companion and probably his closest friend, had gone to bed early, so the lights had likely been out in their wing since ten o'clock or so.

Fitz and Clara were staying in the large separate guest house — which was actually the original house on the property — so Lana would be alone in the north wing of the main house. She should have been comfortable with it — in fact, she *was* very used to it, since at least three or four nights a week she had the mansion practically to herself, with its multitude of bedrooms, sitting rooms and other various spaces for practically every conceivable purpose. She often relished the solitude, after needing to be 'on' for so much of her charity work, which was no easy feat for a natural introvert who would have been happy just reading and drinking tea. Tonight, though, she felt a pang of loneliness.

Before she knew it, they'd pulled up to her front doors. They were tall, made from a thick, dark wood, and the whole impressive entryway looked forbidding, shrouded in darkness.

"They don't leave the front lights on for you?" Mac asked, breaking the silence and some of the tension.

Lana wished they did, but they weren't that kind of family. "I often get home late, and my grandfather is surprisingly frugal, so..." She shrugged, looking away. "I'm accustomed to it." She could feel Mac's gaze, but she refused to turn toward him. "I go in the side door, anyway."

Before she could tell him not to, Mac had gotten out of the car and come around to open her door, offering her his arm. He still looked impossibly handsome in the fading moonlight. It was so cold at the tail end of mid-November that his breath puffed out of his mouth in white clouds, but he looked unruffled in his pristine dress uniform.

"Let me walk you there?" he asked. When she hesitated, with one leg on the ground and one still in the car, he spoke again. "So I'm certain you're safe."

With a swift bolt of comprehension, Lana realized he must be doing this — ensuring her safety — for Fitz, as a favor to her brother, which made total sense. They hadn't totally repaired their relationship as brother and sister, since that would take a long time, but they'd made some good headway, and Fitz had always been protective of her when they had been younger. *So why do I feel so disappointed?* she wondered.

"Since you insist," she agreed, unable to keep the snap of annoyance from her voice entirely. Still, holding onto Mac's solid, warm arm, inhaling his distinctive scent, so smooth and comforting, like masculine soap and cinnamon and detergent, she wasn't sorry not to be alone. No…it was more than that. She wasn't sorry that Mac was the specific man she walked with.

Across the lawn, she saw a light come on in the guest house, which she recognized was in baby Hope's room. Silhouetted on the shades, she saw a curvy woman's figure rocking a child, and a larger outline as a man came up behind her, enveloping them in his shadow with a hug and leading them away from the window. The peace and serenity of the domestic scene, along with recollections of the love that she'd seen on their faces every time Fitz and Clara looked at each other and at tiny, perfect Hope, made her heart hurt, because she knew she would never have anything like it—and didn't deserve it, anyway. Tears filled her eyes. As their steps slowed when they neared the side entrance to her area of the house, she kept her face averted from Mac so he wouldn't see.

"I'm here safely, so you can report back to Fitz that you did your duty," she answered, more coldly than she'd intended.

"Hey, now," Mac answered, turning toward her in front of the side steps and urging her chin up with one strong but gentle finger so he could look at her face. "I never do anything I don't want to do—not anymore, in any case—and I wanted to see you to your door safely for myself, so *I* wouldn't worry." He studied her, and she had the uncomfortable sensation that he saw much more than she'd wanted. "Are those tears, sugar?"

"No," she denied in a thick voice, but her body immediately betrayed her as two droplets fell from her lashes and traced icy paths down her cheeks.

"Oh, darlin', I'm sorry. Not quite sure what I did or said, but I never meant to make you cry," he murmured in a deep, sincere voice, and Lana thought that she could have forgiven him just about anything, if there'd been something to forgive.

"It's not you," she answered. "It's just that I feel so...*alone* sometimes, you know?" she admitted.

"God, yes," he replied, with feeling. He wrapped his arms around her and pulled her close into his body, so tightly that something he had pinned to his uniform pressed into her cheek. In spite of the tiny prick of pain, she felt safer and warmer than she had for a long, long while. "You're not alone now, Lana."

She tipped her head back, and she wasn't sure whether she pushed up toward him first or he lowered his head, but somehow he closed his mouth over hers, and it was sublime. At first, his lips were gentle — surprisingly soft for such a brave, tough ex-military pilot — but when she moaned, he deepened the kiss, and she savored his spicy taste, a little like the coffee they'd drunk at the police station, but mostly just his own unique flavor.

She pushed herself against him, feeling his hardness rise, thick and long, against her stomach, and he tangled his hands into her updo, dislodging bobby pins, which made tiny metallic pings as they landed on the steps. He caressed her tongue with his, claiming her mouth in bold strokes until her nipples tightened against his chest as she imagined how he would claim her with other parts of his body.

When he finally raised his mouth from hers, his breathing harsh and uneven, she noticed they must have walked together right up to the wall of the house, and her back was cold against the bricks. The rapid puffs of her breath mingled with the clouds of his, and he leaned his forehead against hers.

"I'm sorry... I got a little carried away," Mac said, and they still stood so close that she could feel the quick rise and fall of his chest against her breasts.

"No, no...I was just as into it, maybe more," she said, then flushed with embarrassment. "I didn't mean...well, you know. I'm sure you could tell that I was enjoying it, but of course we shouldn't have done that."

Mac took a step back. "What do you mean?"

Lana bit her lip, feeling like she wished the ground would swallow her up. Where some handy quicksand when you needed it?

"Well, like you said, I'm sorry, too."

Mac shook his head. "No, darlin', I'm not sorry it happened...only sorry we went so fast."

When she looked up into his face—so handsome, perfectly formed with strong lines and eyes that she couldn't make out clearly right now in the low light but that she knew were a startling deep green and probably blazing with emotion—she wished she dared to trust herself again with a good man, a kind man, a true friend like Mac. Being with someone like him wasn't in the cards for her, though. That kind of man wanted more than she could give—more than she was capable of giving anymore.

She put her hand on his chest. "Mac, there can't be anything more between us. I can't be with someone like you." She tried to be gentle, but she rushed her words as thick tears rose in her throat.

Mac took another step back, breaking all contact between them. "Someone like me, huh? Why did I think you were different?" His voice was hollow, resigned...but the tone was underlaid with hurt.

"That's not—" she started to explain, but he cut her off.

"You know what, Lana? Don't say anything you might regret. I'll stay away from you, and you can stay away from me from now on, but no matter what, we'll still have to see each other sometimes, and I don't want it to be any worse than it has to be."

Lana felt as if he'd slapped her, but she forgave him for lashing out. He didn't understand, but explaining might make it more painful. As Fitz's closest friend, he *was* bound to cross her path in the future at important events.

"If that's what you want," she agreed, her voice low and sad.

"Does it matter what I want?" Mac's laugh was mirthless, and he started to turn away. "No, hold on. I'm gonna say one more thing first, because I vowed that if I ever started to feel for someone again, I would say the words out loud — not leave confusion or doubt."

Lana braced herself for whatever he was going to say, but his words were more surprising for their tenderness than anything else.

"It sounds like we don't feel the same way and maybe you won't thank me for saying this, but no matter how you feel, I care about you. I was beginnin' to think I might be able to care pretty deeply and that maybe you could, too."

She winced at the raw tone of his voice.

"That doesn't change overnight. Truth is, for a man like me, that doesn't really change, *period*. So if you're ever in trouble or hurting — no matter everything we said tonight — you can call me and I'll be there. That's it."

His offer stunned her, and letting him turn around and walk away, back into the darkness that was beginning to streak gray with the first light of the coming dawn, was one of the worst things she'd ever forced herself to do. He'd be better off without her, though. She knew it, and he'd recognize it, too, in time.

She'd thought her sad, shredded heart was incapable of feeling anything anymore, but now she learned — too late — that she must have been mistaken. If it had truly been destroyed, it couldn't hurt so darn bad now. She hurried inside the massive house, her steps echoing off the walls and floors of the empty rooms, and cried for everything that might have been.

Chapter Two

Five months later

"Good evening, Miss Lana. Punctual, as usual." The approval in Roger's voice was unmistakable. "May I take your wrap?"

The absurdity of her grandfather's butler's formality when she had just walked over from one wing of the house to another wasn't lost on her. She nearly smiled when she thought of how much Mac would appreciate it if he were here. He'd told her that he genuinely liked both of the older gentlemen. Her burgeoning smile turned to a frown, and she pushed the thought out of her head. *You promised that you wouldn't mope anymore,* she reminded herself.

"It's quite cozy, I can promise you," Roger assured her, interpreting her hesitation as concern—justified by prior visits—that her grandfather would have the thermostat set to a temperature that could charitably be called 'brisk'. The older manservant leaned over conspiratorially. "I convinced your grandfather that we'd better light a fire tonight, given the damp conditions—better for the photographs, you know." The few photos that remained of her grandmother, Flora, were her grandfather's prize possessions. "He even turned the thermostat up to...*sixty-three*." The last words were so low they were barely a whisper.

Lana's eyebrows shot up in surprise. "Is he feeling worse?"

Her grandfather's cackle rang out from the other room. "As if! You'll not be inheriting my fortune just yet, missy, so don't sound so hopeful," he called with feeling. Even after all his years in Minnesota, his voice still held a hint of his Irish accent, especially when he was worked up.

Guess he still has ears like a bat, she thought wryly.

"I'm fit as a fiddle, and that's the truth, but I did think I saw a spot of condensation on the frame of one of the pictures of my darlin' Flora, and I'll have no more of that, thank you very much." The sound her grandad made next could only be described as a guttural *harrumph*. "Now hurry up and give your shawl to Roger so we can eat. I'm so hungry my stomach is gnawing at my backbone!"

Sliding her scarlet cashmere pashmina off her shoulders, she rolled her eyes at Roger, who kept his face impassive as he took it from her. The butler couldn't keep the twinkle from his eyes, though. Lana was certain...*absolutely positive*...that her grandfather had had his massive afternoon tea a scant two hours earlier, since she'd seen their chef, Marcel, laying it on the tray in the kitchen. She was happy to humor her grandfather, though.

"I'm coming, Granda. Can't have you wasting away on my watch, can we? And at our Sunday dinner, no less? Drew and Colin would never forgive me." As always, she took a deep breath when she crossed into the living room, marveling at how it still smelled exactly as it always had for as long as she could remember, warm and comforting, with hints of pipe tobacco and her grandmother's floral perfume, even though she had been gone for a number of years and her grandfather had long since given up smoking.

In spite of his relatively small stature—made a bit shorter and slighter by his advanced age—even ensconced in his favorite armchair under a thick plaid blanket, Pat Fitzhugh remained an incredibly commanding man. As a child, she'd watched grown men stumble over their words when he challenged them, and she'd heard folks whisper in awe whenever he walked by. She crossed the length of the plush carpet to where he sat and leaned over to kiss one of his papery cheeks. She didn't like how his recent illness had been lingering, making him even paler than he had been.

"Good evening, Granda. I won't bother to inquire how you're feeling, since you're obviously in rare form tonight."

He drew his bushy white eyebrows together, looking peeved that she'd taken the wind out of his sails. "Well, I'm fine, I suppose, even if my arthritis has been acting up a bit. No need to hover over me like the angel of death just yet, m'dear. Step back so I can see you better."

Lana obligingly took one large step backward, nearly colliding with the silent Roger, who had snuck up without her noticing. Long ago, she'd resigned herself to never knowing how the man had acquired his truly astonishing stealth, but she secretly suspected a background with the CIA, MI6 or something similar. He deftly sidestepped her, coming to perch in a dignified manner on the edge of the chair next to her grandfather's.

"Peaky, a bit pale…" Pat shook his head and pursed his lips. "You're absolutely correct, Roger. She's lost some of her sparkle."

This time, Lana couldn't contain her huff of shocked laughter.

"No need to hold back, Granda. Tell me what you really think." For someone used to constantly being on display and looking her best, the negative comment coming from a member of her own family stung.

"I'm certain your grandfather doesn't mean to say you aren't as lovely as ever, Miss Lana." Roger's softly spoken compliment warmed her.

Shaking his hand dismissively, her grandfather continued. "Of course, you're still a rare beauty, like your mother and your grandmother. Anyone would be a fool not to see *that*," he said peevishly. "But your joy, Lana…all that extra shine you had a few months ago has all but faded away. Did something happen with that blond Southern fellow, the pilot? Friend of Colin's, wasn't he?"

It never ceased to amaze her how her grandfather seemed to see absolutely everything. Lana felt a hot flush creep up her neck and into her cheeks and ears. With her fair skin, she knew she must be a blazing pink color. She looked away in embarrassment, not eager in the slightest to talk to either Granda or Roger about what had happened that night with Mac. Her focus caught on the television, a discreetly placed large flatscreen across the room, which flickered with the nightly news, the closed-captioning that her grandfather and Roger favored scrolling across the bottom.

Footage of a familiar house made her freeze. As the newscaster's comments flashed white against the black text boxes, the blood drained out of her cheeks, and she felt her lips go cold.

"Turn…turn on the volume," she croaked.

Her grandfather grumbled, but Roger did as she'd asked just in time for her to hear the end of the story.

"Tragically, both Mr. Erasmus and his wife, Samantha, were pronounced dead at the hospital. They are survived only by their three-year-old son. Mrs. Erasmus, famous for her charitable foundation, was also the sole remaining member of the Jemison manufacturing dynasty." Here, the newscaster paused before continuing. "And now we go to Hilary Swanson, who's in Blaine tonight with a feel-good story of a little boy who just wanted to help his elderly neighbor, a Vietnam veteran, shovel his driveway…"

The television screen went black as someone shut it off, and Lana felt the pressure of Roger's hand on her elbow as he guided her to sit down in the pink velvet chair her grandmother had favored.

"Tragic news, indeed. I'm so sorry, m'dear." Her grandfather's voice was grave and sympathetic. When she darted a glance at him, he looked older…and frailer. It made Lana remember that he was a man who had buried his two sons and one daughter-in-law, along with his beloved wife and countless other friends and family members over the years. "I remember meeting Cain Erasmus a few times, and of course little Sam Jemison was here practically every day for years. I never understood why she never came to visit you after she changed schools."

I know why. The familiar stab of regret and shame hit her low in her gut, but even worse than usual. Sam had been her best friend, so close they'd been like sisters. As if conjured by her thoughts, a memory of Sam, giggling uncontrollably as they pretended to be mermaids, her carroty-red hair glinting in the June sunshine and her blue eyes shining with tears of mirth, popped into Lana's mind. *Oh, Sam,* she thought, and the living room became blurry.

"Sam was...wonderful." Her voice shook. "They both were. My God, I'm...stunned."

Roger patted her shoulder. When she felt the vibration of her phone and looked down at the caller ID, at first she just gaped, uncomprehending. It read 'Sam Home'. How was that even possible? She'd never deleted her friend's contact info, moving it from her old phone to her new one, always hopeful over the past twelve years that she'd someday have the chance to apologize and make things right...but this must be some kind of sick joke.

From where he was still standing next to her, Roger must have been able to see the screen of her mobile, as well as sense her confusion. He smiled gently. "It looks as if someone from her home might be trying to reach you."

*Of course...*of course *it's someone else, calling from Sam's house,* she realized, releasing the breath she hadn't known she'd been holding.

When Lana clicked the green button to answer, an older woman's voice came over the line.

"Hello, Lana? Is that you?" She sounded rough, as though she'd been crying, but the voice was still so familiar that it made Lana's heart squeeze in her chest.

"Mrs. Schultz?" she answered, knowing that she was correct and picturing the tall, brown-haired housekeeper who had been softly rounded but possessed a backbone of steel. "Yes, it's Lana...Lana Fitzhugh. We just saw the news. I am so deeply sorry.

Words aren't enough to tell you how sorry I am…if that's why you were calling." Speaking to the older woman who had worked for Sam's family as long as Lana had known Sam, Lana felt as if she were an awkward fourteen-year-old again.

"Thank you, Lana. The tragedy…" Mrs. Schultz took in a shaky breath. "Telling you was part of why I was calling, but there's something else."

"Okay," Lana answered, at a loss. *What else could there be?*

"Samantha—" The older woman's voice broke, and sympathy welled up inside of Lana.

"It's all right. You don't have to tell me now," Lana assured her. "I can come over tomorrow morning…or whenever is best."

"No, no…that's the thing, dear. Cain and Samantha have no living relatives—well, none that they trust, anyway—so Samantha made me swear to call you if-if anything ever happened to both of them. She said you knew…that you'd promised."

Lana's mind raced. Growing up, Sam had a terrible home life, and Lana had promised, long ago, to take care of anything for her friend if something happened to her. Lana had solemnly vowed to protect any pets or children, and Sam had done the same for Lana.

"Their little boy?" she asked, clutching her phone tightly against her ear in a death-grip.

"That's right. Grayson…but they always call—*called* him Gray. I stayed last night, but I'm getting on a bit now and my husband had surgery a month ago…" The housekeeper sounded distraught.

"I completely understand, Mrs. Schultz. Nobody would ever question your dedication," Lana murmured in a soothing tone.

"Thank you," the older woman answered in a watery voice. "So, the official reading of their legal documents will confirm everything, but Cain and Samantha's last wishes were that you become Grayson's legal guardian."

If Lana hadn't already been sitting down, she would have fallen over. As if in fast-forward, memory after memory of Sam streamed through her mind. Her friend had never wanted to talk much about what little family she had, but she had seemed nervous about them and seriously leery of most domestic employees. Mrs. Schultz had been the only exception. With an adult's insight, Lana could see that Sam had been afraid and must have been hurt at some point. At the time, Lana had happily agreed to the far-off possibility of taking care of Sam's future dream-children, and she could still remember the relief in her friend's wide eyes, fringed with distinctive dark-red eyelashes. *Always*...they had always promised to be there for each other, no matter what. Lana had done a terrible thing, and she'd thought she'd ruined their friendship forever, but had Sam forgiven her—or was this just a mistake from an outdated document?

With sudden clarity, Lana realized that it didn't matter. She had promised Sam, and a Fitzhugh never broke a promise. After that one disastrous teenage night when she'd ruined everything, Lana had vowed to be the best version of herself she could possibly be. She would be proud to honor Sam and Cain by becoming guardian to their son, Grayson. *Gray*.

"I'll pack a couple things and be there within the hour," she confirmed.

Chapter Three

Lana flopped down onto the large leather couch, wincing as her tired leg muscles connected with the soft cushions.

"Oh, good Lord, how the heck does everyone make this look so easy on TV? I swear, running after Gray at the playground is more intense than two of the spin classes I used to do at the fancy gym downtown." Lana heard Clara's laugh, rich and full-bodied, from the other side of the room, but she was too tired to sit up to look at her future sister-in-law just yet.

"He was pretty...intense." Clara settled onto the loveseat across from Lana, arranging pillows and clothing to start to nurse Hope, which Lana watched from a sideways perspective. "I mean, I had no idea three-year-olds could run that fast. When you stopped to help me lay out that blanket for Hope, he was halfway across the whole field in, like, four seconds."

Lana chuckled at the memory. She'd been frantic at the time, sprinting to catch up to his ridiculously speedy little form, but now she was impressed. "It was great to see him animated like that. He's been pretty somber and reserved most of the time. He really did fly, didn't he?"

"Like the wind," Clara agreed. "Did he wake up when you put him into bed?"

Lana shook her head, forcing herself to shift into an upright position, even if she was still a little slumped. "Nope, he barely twitched as I carried him from the car straight to naptime, and I didn't hear a peep when I latched the door." Since Gray could climb out of his bed, she was careful to always latch the childproof doorknob so he couldn't escape on his own and wander around the large house unsupervised.

"He was probably exhausted! How many times did he ask you to hold him up so he could cross those monkey-bar thingies?"

Lana knew what part of the playground equipment her brother's fiancée referred to...like a modern, blue version of the monkey bars they'd played with as children. "Ugh, seven, and my biceps will never be the same," she groaned, but she smiled as she recalled how happy Gray had looked after each successful crossing. The little boy could use all the stolen moments of happiness he could get.

"How is he doing? How are *you* doing with all this? It's been such a huge adjustment in the past ten days." Clara's hazel eyes held true concern, and Lana felt a wave of affection for her brother's wife-to-be. Colin — who she needed to mentally remember to call Fitz — was lucky to have found himself such a wonderful partner. Lana was grateful that Clara was fast becoming one of her closest friends.

Lana gave the question careful consideration. "It's been challenging for both of us, I suppose, although, of course, more so for Gray. I think that the funeral helped, even though it was insanely difficult." Lana thought back to the service, just a blur of grief and mourning, and sly whispers from a few former schoolmates about her wild teenage reputation. She'd thought she'd left those mostly behind, but she should have known better.

"At first, he was just confused and didn't seem to understand that his parents weren't coming home, but I think that seeing all the mourners, and the coffins, along with the beautiful memorial that Cain's close friend had put together, allowed him to start to grieve in his own way. Mrs. Schultz being here definitely helped, too, although her husband took a turn for the worse, so she has had to take a few weeks off. She left yesterday. Gray kind of yo-yos between seeming like a regular preschooler to being super anxious and clingy, but apparently that's really typical."

Clara nodded, stroking baby Hope's head, now covered with a growing cap of gleaming auburn curls, so like her mother's. "Yeah, grief for little kids is so hard. I'm glad he has you. Did he, um, know who you were?"

Lana appreciated Clara's attempt at delicacy. "Yes, I guess Sam spoke of me enough that he recognized me... She even, uh—" Lana's throat went thick with tears so that she had to clear it. "She even kept a framed picture of the two of us on the wall of her office, and Gray went and pointed to it when I arrived. He called me 'Auntie Lala'." The recollection of that and the knowledge that, even after all the time that had passed, her friend had apparently not hated her—*because you don't keep a framed 11x17 picture of someone you loathe, right?*—touched her, deeply. For about the hundredth time since she'd learned of Sam's death, she wished she'd had the courage to reach out sooner, to try to make peace before it had been too late.

The warmth of Clara's expression reached her from all the way across the room, along with the empathy in it. "That's really good. I'm so glad to hear that, Lana, especially since I know things were…strained between you for a while."

It was both a statement and a gentle question, but something Lana truly appreciated about Clara was that she was an awesome listener but she never pushed.

The silence that fell between them for a moment was comfortable, and Clara lifted baby Hope from her breast to her shoulder. The little girl gave a baby-sigh of such contentment that it made Lana's eyes prickle with moisture, which turned into tears of mirth when her niece belched loudly enough to put a room full of pre-teen boys at a sleepover to shame.

Clara patted her daughter's back. "Well then, I bet you feel better now, huh?" she said, giggling.

"How did that much gas fit into her little body?" Lana asked, snorting with laughter.

"I know!" Clara agreed. "Mac says that his middle niece was the same way, and she's a delightful seven-year-old now, so at least I have confirmation from a real-world source that it's normal."

At the mention of Mac's name, Lana tensed. True to his promise on the night of the gala, he'd stayed away from her except when they'd been forced to cross paths at the engagement party for Fitz and Clara. There, Mac had been pleasant and cordial, and her heart had ached so much that it hurt her soul.

"How — how is he?" Lana blurted the question before she could stop herself.

Clara didn't hide her surprise very well, but she was quick to answer. "He's okay. Actually, he's on vacation for a few weeks down in Georgia, staying with his younger sister. Pat told him to feel free to take some time."

The keen interest Lana felt was entirely inappropriate. "Oh?" she said, trying and failing to sound casual.

"He's seemed sort of…unsettled lately—like maybe he's trying to figure out his next step," Clara speculated, but Lana knew that her future sister-in-law's intuition was usually spot on.

"Do you—do you think he's going to move back there? To Georgia?" Lana asked, feeling curiously breathless. She hadn't realized how much she'd liked knowing that Mac was nearby, or at least just a quick flight away on one of her family's private jets, as long as he worked for her grandfather.

"Hard to say… You know how mysterious he can be." Clara's expression grew intent, and probing. "Don't you?"

Before she could formulate a response, Lana heard a light *thump-thump-thump*, almost like the slight weight of something falling. It sounded like it was coming from the grand front staircase…the one that Gray was forbidden to use by himself. Bile rose from her stomach to her throat and a feeling of sick dread lodged there as she shot to her feet.

"Gray," she breathed, running for the stairs. She heard Clara following quickly behind her.

His little body lay crumpled on the upper landing of the marble staircase, and she gave a wordless cry of horror. Without conscious thought, she sprinted up the stairs to him with nearly inhuman speed, mindless with fear.

When she'd nearly reached him, every possible awful outcome playing out in her head, he suddenly sat up, shaking his head. When he saw her kneel down next to him, a welcoming smile spread across his face.

"Lala," he called happily. He always called her that since 'Lana' was hard for him to say. "I came to find you!"

She wrapped him in her arms and pulled him to her, helpless to do otherwise with the force of her relief.

"Are you okay, Gray? I think you fell... Does anything hurt?" She managed to release him enough so that she could run her hands all over him, but he didn't wince or seem to be in any pain.

"I fell down the stairs, but nothing hurts." He took a deep breath and shrugged. "Nope, I'm okay!"

At his utterly normal response, she felt her eyes prickle with tears of relief as she crushed him to her again. She looked up at Clara, who had come to stand next to her.

"Do you think he's really all right?" she asked. Clara wasn't a doctor, but she had helped her father and brother treat a lot of patients, including Fitz, when Clara had found him injured and unconscious in the woods near her cabin.

"I mean, he does seem pretty normal now, and kids are super tough. Maybe he just got the wind knocked out of him? We can always call Gray's pediatrician, or Lars, if you'd prefer."

Clara's brother, Lars, had come from northern Minnesota a number of times to visit, and Lana had really liked him every time they'd met.

Lana bit her lip. "I don't want to worry anyone, but do you think Lars would mind?"

Laughing, Clara dug her phone out of her pocket, even as she held baby Hope up with her other arm in a move that Lana thought was a total pro-mom maneuver. "Oh my gosh, no! If you knew how many times Fitz and I called him about Hope, especially over the first few months…" She looked sheepish. "But Lars always says that he doesn't worry about the parents who call a lot. He worries about the ones who never do."

"Belly! How are you? I thought you were visiting the glamorous Lana today?" Lars' rich voice boomed out of the speaker on Clara's phone, and Lana blushed.

"Um, I am *still* visiting the glamorous Lana, and you're on a video call with both of us, actually. We think Gray took a little tumble down the stairs."

Clara turned the phone toward Lana, and she saw Lars' movie-star-handsome face. If she hadn't cared for Mac so much, even if she knew that she wasn't good enough for him, her head would certainly have been turned by Clara's brother. Lars had the kind of perfect good looks that made people do a double-take, and in addition to how attractive he was, he was unfailingly kind, friendly and caring. However, he kind of gave off a subtly distant vibe with almost everyone except Clara.

"Do you mind taking a look?" Lana asked hesitantly. "The front staircase — which we always try to avoid with Gray — is marble."

And how the heck did Gray get out of his room? she wondered, able to think more clearly now that the worst of the scare seemed to have passed. She had a distinct memory of closing the door until the latch clicked, and she knew he couldn't open the child-proofed doorknob. For heaven's sake, *she* had trouble opening it as an adult.

"Of course I don't mind, as long as you understand that I really can't give an official opinion over the phone…which my little sister forgets sometimes." Lars' laugh was rich and full.

"Understood. I just really appreciate it. I'm so new to all this." Lana gestured generally at the stairway and Gray. "I don't want to drag Gray into the doctor for something silly."

"No problem," Lars answered, then his bedside manner seemed to take over. "Belly, can you show me the patient? How does he seem now?"

Clara held her phone while Lana felt all over Gray's head, finding a small red bump but nothing more, and examined his pupils, which seemed normal. When he started squirming in her grip to be released, she let him run to the spacious family room where, thanks to the open floor plan, they could still see him.

"If you have any concerns at all, take him in to see his pediatrician, but based on your description and how he seemed just now, I would guess that he's going to be fine. Just watch for any changes in behavior, unusual sleepiness, change in pupil size…all the warning signs we just talked about. If you see any of those, take him straight to the ER."

"Of course," Lana agreed without hesitation. "Thank you so much for putting my mind more at ease. I just… I really don't want to do the wrong thing," she admitted.

Clara smiled understandingly. "I think all us new parents feel the same way," she said, and Lana was warmed by her tone.

A short while later, after they'd hung up with Lars and they'd all returned to the family room where Gray had a play kitchen and supermarket set up in the corner, Clara frowned at a message she received on her phone.

"Bad news?" Lana asked.

"Oh, no…just your crazy brother. He's itching to head back to the cabin early and wants to leave tonight, but I don't want to just up and run out of here," Clara answered, her eyes soft when she spoke about Fitz.

Lana hurried to reassure her immediately. "Oh my gosh, don't worry about it! You heard Lars, Gray is fine, and I'll be fine too, once my heart slows down to normal. You should get a head start back to your fancy 'love cabin'," she teased.

Clara's answering snort made baby Hope twitch in her sleep. "Ah, fancy love cabin is not exactly an accurate description." She giggled. "Did I mention there's no running water? Unless you count a water pump as running?" She sighed dreamily, obviously remembering. "But it will still be pretty romantic to watch the sunset on the lake together again...as a family this time."

"It's a *Looooove Cabiiiiin*. I rest my case," Lana returned with a saucy wink, drawing out the syllables until they were something silly, and Clara tossed a small throw pillow at her head. Lana ducked it easily.

"Well, only if you're sure?" Clara asked, but Lana could tell that her future sister-in-law was hoping to go.

"I'm sure. And you'd probably better get home before he starts packing for Hope. You know that he'll fill, like, twelve suitcases until you guys will have to bring a spare SUV just for her luggage."

Clara laughed but drew her dark-red eyebrows together and bit her bottom lip. "Oh my gosh, you're totally right. I can't even trust Fitz to pack her diaper bag, because he goes into crazy dad mode and tries to think through every potential contingency. I end up with six bottles, twelve outfits, a whole package of diapers and a full picnic lunch for myself. Try to walk *that* around the zoo." She sighed, but it was a loving sound. "He even wanted me to bring a whole bag of food here today, as if you were planning to *starve* me. Wild man."

Lana chuckled. It was true that her normally level-headed brother became an insane worrywart when it came to Clara and Hope, and while it was sweet to watch, she couldn't imagine how his fiancée put up with it. "Wild for you and Hope," she agreed. "Gray and I will walk you to your car."

Gray and Lana kissed baby Hope's forehead before Clara secured the infant in the backseat of the massive SUV that Fitz insisted Clara drive because it was bulletproof and reinforced like a tank.

As she watched Clara check all the straps of the baby seat, Lana felt an uncomfortable crawling sensation on the back of her neck, as if she were being watched. No, more than that…as if the watcher hated her. She turned to glance at the trees but saw nothing out of the ordinary.

They hugged Clara goodbye quickly, and as soon as she drove away, Lana hurried Gray back into the house, making sure to set the house alarm behind them and deadbolt the doors.

Chapter Four

It had only been four days since Clara's visit, but it felt like four years, and Lana wondered — not for the first time — just where she'd gone wrong. While Gray had previously been having a hard time processing his grief, he'd still been relatively even-tempered, all things considered. However, since that afternoon with Clara, something had changed, and she wasn't sure how to fix it. Worse, she worried that she couldn't predict when something else would go wrong, and it terrified her. Now, at least temporarily alone for a moment of quiet in her bedroom, she mentally reviewed everything that had happened, trying to make sense of it, to find some sort of solution.

First, Gray had started having terrible nightmares. She'd sprinted into his room at least six times the night of Clara's visit after she'd put him to bed, and each time found the preschooler a trembling, sobbing mess, pointing frantically at the corners of his bedroom and saying he saw monsters and ghosts. Lana had patiently checked every corner, under the bed and in the closet, but he'd remained inconsolable until she'd agreed to lie down next to him until he fell asleep again. Still, it seemed like practically as soon as she snuck out and left him alone, collapsing onto her own bed, she was awoken again by his screaming.

After that first overnight, she'd figured it was just a fluke. Anyone could be occasionally sleepless or have bad dreams. But it had continued for the past three nights, and now both she and Gray could barely keep their eyes open. She'd taken Gray to see his pediatrician, who had basically told her that it was totally normal for a three-year-old who had had such a traumatic event happen to have nightmares and to act clingy. She'd come away from the appointment feeling silly and inadequate as a guardian—and even more exhausted than she'd been before they'd made the trip across town.

Still, if it had just been the constant night terrors and sleeplessness, she could have dealt with it. Other weird things had started to happen, too, though…and that odd feeling, like a trickle of cold water down her spine, that someone or something was watching her, never seemed to go away.

The morning after Clara's visit, she'd messed up and must have put in the wrong cook time for Gray's oatmeal into the microwave. She would've sworn she had taken the thick plastic bowl out and set it on the table before going to get him from the other room, but when she'd returned, the steaming dish had still been in the microwave. Thank goodness she'd remembered, even in her sleep-deprived fog, to check the warm mixture by tasting a spoonful because she'd nearly burned a hole through her tongue. She still didn't have any tastebuds in one spot, and if she'd given the mixture to Gray, he could have seriously hurt himself.

The next day, when she had run him his nightly bath, she had a distinct memory of assessing the temperature with her elbow, just as she always did, before going to undress him and bring him into the bathroom. She thanked heaven for whatever impulse had made her check a second time because the water had been so hot she'd scalded her elbow and cried out in pain, jumping back so fast she'd nearly hit her head on the bathroom sink. For Gray's sake, she'd pretended to be fine and had just quietly drained the tub before carefully refilling it, gauging the temperature over and over again as the water level rose, but the incident had rattled her. It made her wonder what the heck was going on with her that she—always so detailed to the point of being called uptight—was forgetting things left and right.

Then, earlier today, she'd somehow forgotten to lock the back door. No…it was worse than that. When she'd gone looking for Gray for dinner, the back door had been wide open. Luckily, she'd caught up to him before he'd gotten halfway across the grass, but her heart still started to pound, even now, at the remembered terror. She wished she could have traced the action to one of the staff who came in during the day, but she'd reviewed the security logs and she and Gray had been alone at the time, and there had been no unusual attempts at entry.

Now, lying in her bed, so exhausted that her eyelids felt as if they were filled with coarse sand, the connection between the issues seemed clear. They didn't just have to do with her… *She* was the cause of them. She'd overheated the oatmeal, she'd let the water get way too hot for the bath and now there had been two times that she hadn't closed or locked doors. *Maybe I'm having a mental breakdown?* she wondered. *But wouldn't I feel like I was having a mental breakdown? Then again, maybe that's what everyone who is having some sort of psychological break thinks?*

She flipped onto her other side so she faced the wall, torn between the syrupy abyss of sleep that pulled at her and the need to consider this more carefully. *What is safest for Gray? Should I go to a mental health care facility for evaluation?*

Before she could come to a decision, she heard the now-familiar cry of terror from the other room and hauled her tired body to her feet as quickly as she could. As she stumbled into his bedroom, he was curled up into the farthest corner of his bed, shaking with terror.

"It's okay, baby. I'm here. Lala's here," she crooned, sitting down gently so as not to scare him more. As soon as she was fully seated, he flung himself into her arms, and she hugged him tightly.

"The...m-m-monster. Waiting...for...me...right...over...there." Gray was crying so hard he was gasping for breath. Still, even though it shook, his hand clearly pointed to one of the corners of the room. It was the same one she'd checked so many times over the past few nights that it had become like a routine.

"Okay, sweetie. I think it was just another bad dream. Let me go take a look. I'll turn on your dino lamp so we can see that there isn't anything there, all right?"

Gray sniffled and hiccupped but nodded his agreement, moving back a scant inch from her. She leaned over to pull the brachiosaurus's tail and the room was filled with a dim, greenish light.

Dutifully, she lumbered to her feet, feeling almost three times her age, and went to the corner in question.

"See?" she started. "There's nothing—" she broke off mid-sentence, something sparkly catching her eye. Something…oddly familiar.

"There's nothing?" Gray asked in a small, worried voice.

She knelt down, trying to feel confident, all the while a dull feeling of dread grew larger in her gut until it threatened to consume her. "That's right, baby. See? I'm touching the rug and there is definitely no monster here." As she ran her hand over the thick carpeting, her fingers closed over a familiar shape. It was her grandmother's favorite diamond brooch in the shape of a hummingbird—the same brooch that Lana had thought she'd lost, along with her thin spring coat, four days earlier. Her mind raced. *What. The. Hell?*

"Okay, Lala," Gray agreed, his sweet little voice in the silence nearly making her jump. "Lie down with me 'til I fall back asleep?"

Lana's heart felt like it physically twisted in her chest. How could he not see that *she* might be the monster? *Oh, God, is it even safe for me to stay until he sleeps? Should I call the police? What would I tell them?* She took a deep breath to steady herself. Whatever was going on, she felt lucid now, and she trusted that she would never—*never, ever*—hurt the little boy who was staring so trustingly at her with his eyes just like Sam's, right down to the dark-red eyelashes.

"Okay, baby. Scooch over. I need more room than that!" she joked, and the ghost of a smile touched his lips. He made room and she curled next to him, her thoughts buzzing like hornets as he slowly relaxed back to sleep.

Who should I call? If I call the police or the fire department, will they believe me? Oh, hello officers, I think that I'm having a psychotic break and menacing the small child in my care, but I can't exactly remember or prove it. What would happen to Gray then? Her stomach felt sick with worry. She thought of calling Fitz and Clara, but they were at the cabin for some much-needed family time, and they would have spotty cell service. Drew was at an important business conference in Munich, and her grandfather seemed to have had a bit of a relapse and had been feeling particularly unwell this week. *No...absolutely not.* She didn't want to worry her family, especially since she'd only just gotten all of them to see her as more than a spoiled, hysterical teenager. She wasn't in a hurry to lose that progress.

Unbidden, the memory of Mac's parting words to her all those months earlier came back to her. *If you're ever in trouble or hurting — no matter everything we said tonight — you can call me and I'll be there. That's it.*

Did he mean that? she wondered. Even as she thought the question, she knew the answer. *Heck, yes, he meant it.* Mac was many things, but he held his honor sacred, and that was nothing short of a promise. Even if it were only for Fitz's sake, Mac would help her. *He wouldn't be doing it only for Fitz,* a small voice that sounded suspiciously like her conscience insisted on reminding her, but she brushed it aside. It didn't matter why he helped, only that he did.

Untangling herself from Gray's small form, no small feat with his limbs so heavy from sleep, she crept into the hallway and dug out her phone. With tears streaming down her face, she searched for the entry for

Mac's number on her phone, which she had never been able to bring herself to delete, and pressed the green Call button.

* * * *

It was a damn steamy night for late spring, even in Georgia, and Mac felt restless...like the sheets were too damp, the air too thick, the scents of the flowers his younger sister, Jenna, loved to plant all around the house too strong, almost overwhelming. Sighing, he freed his legs from the ropes that the sheets had curled themselves into and put his hands behind his head. If he wasn't going to sleep, he might as well try to puzzle things out.

Jenna had cooked all his favorites for dinner, including her light-as-air biscuits and chicken fried steak, finished with a peach cobbler. After dinner, her husband Ray had invited him to share a glass of smoky twenty-year-old whiskey in the library while Jenna settled five-year-old Connor down for the night. His sister's smile — the same one that had seen her named the Peachy Keen Queen at their hometown festival ten years earlier — had never faltered, but he couldn't shake the gut feeling that she wasn't entirely happy. Unfortunately, the death glare she'd flashed at him when he'd opened his mouth to speak before he went off with Ray hadn't exactly been inviting. He vowed to make time to ask her about it when they were alone the next day, after Ray had gone to his job at the local bank.

Turning it over in his mind, Mac knew that vague concern for his younger sister might be part of what was making him uneasy, but it wasn't all of it. No...there in the back of his thoughts, where she always lingered, was Lana Fitzhugh. Still...*always.* She'd been so damn beautiful at Fitz and Clara's engagement party that it had been agony to see her, come so close to her that he could smell her unique scent, hear her low, husky laughter but not be able to touch her. Worse, even though she'd been stunning—because he didn't think she was capable of being otherwise—her eyes had held sadness...and something fragile. If she'd seemed happy, or even content, he told himself that he would have been able to simply wish her well...but vulnerable, Lana called out to his every protective instinct. She'd given him a firm no, and he would respect that, but his body and mind refused to forget her.

I wonder what she's doing right now, he thought, trying to picture her. He'd subtly asked Fitz and Clara about her several times—or maybe not so subtly, judging by the knowing look Clara had flashed him—but in the months since the gala and their kiss, he hadn't heard a whisper about her with another man. The primitive part of him had been happy, but the more realistic part of him argued that she might just be good at hiding her liaisons. And yet, he just didn't feel like she was lost to him, committed to someone else. Instead, some dark, secret part of him still insisted that she was *his*—his to care for, comfort, protect. In spite of her confidence and tireless efforts for the various charities she supported, he'd always—since the first moment they'd met—sensed a kindred spirit in her, someone solitary and wounded but still determined to go on.

He touched his lips as he remembered their first kiss—destined to be their last, it seemed—and how soft she'd felt against him, lush and curved, fitting perfectly. His cock strained in the thin pajama pants, which were all he wore, and he groaned. For months, heavily medicated and in constant pain after his leg had been amputated, he'd worried that he'd never get hard again, never be able to give that part of himself to another lover. With Lana, though, he'd been full and aching since the first moment he'd seen her, in spite of knowing that she was the cherished younger sister of one of his closest friends, on top of being the granddaughter of his employer.

When his phone vibrated on the bedside table and he saw the name on the caller ID, at first he thought that he must have drifted off after all and his dream had conjured Lana's name. The buzzing was insistent, though, and he shook himself out of his stupor to fumble the phone into his hands and up to his ear. Any lingering fog of dreams or desire vanished in an instant at her voice on the other end of the line.

"Mac?" she asked, her tone thick with tears. He felt as if she'd reached through the phone and squeezed his heart right there in his chest.

"Yeah, Lana, I'm here, sugar." He tried to sound calm and reassuring, even while his gut was urging him to run to his car and drive directly to the FBO where one of Pat Fitzhugh's Cessnas was currently hangared.

"I'm sorry... Gosh, it's so late. I didn't realize...and you probably don't want to hear from me, only my brothers are away and Granda hasn't been feeling well..." Her deep breath sounded shaky, like it had almost come out as a sob.

He sat up on the edge of the bed at the wild edge to what she said, taking a deep breath before he answered. "I'm so glad you called me, baby. And I wasn't sleepin', so you didn't wake me...although I wouldn't mind if you had." His mind raced at what could possibly have driven her to call him in the middle of the night after months, but he forced himself to stay cool and logical. Lana needed that from him.

"First of all, are you someplace safe?" He tensed, waiting for her reply. Lana's hysterical bark of laughter was not what he expected.

"I'm safe...or safe enough, I suppose. It's not me I'm worried about, though. It's Gray."

"*Gray?*" Mac congratulated himself on how normal he sounded, given that jealousy was a writhing, seething mass in his gut. Maybe Mac wasn't the right kind of man for her, but it sounded like this Gray — whoever he was — was more appropriate, better, *whole*.

"Yes...things are so messed up that I'm afraid to leave him alone, but I also—" She broke off on a little sob. "I can't trust myself." The last words were barely a whisper, and Mac's heart ached at how broken she sounded. Was she in some sort of abusive relationship?

"Is he there with you now?" The breath faltered in Mac's chest as he waited for her reply. If she was with another man—someone she cared for—would he still be willing to help her? Before the thought even fully formed, Mac dismissed it. Damn straight he would. This was *Lana*. He wanted her safe and happy, no matter who she was with or how she'd hurt his feelings. That didn't mean he wouldn't try to convince her he was the better option, though.

"H-he's in his bedroom, and I'm in the hallway just outside. I'm afraid to leave him alone, even to go to sleep." Her breath hitched, and she sounded breathless. "Mac, something is really wrong, and I think it might be with me."

Every sense he had went on high-alert, and his inner alarm bells began to blare as Mac stiffened. Lana sounded terrified. More than that, she seemed almost afraid of herself.

"I'm coming right now," he said tersely, putting the phone on speaker so he could pull on his prosthetic and grab the small duffel that he'd barely started to unpack. "Just text me the address where you are and give me four hours. Can you hold on that long, darlin'?"

Lana's exhale was shocked. "D-don't you want to know more? About what I might have done?"

"Doesn't matter to me," Mac answered, surprised that it was true. "I trust you, and whatever it is, we'll figure it out."

"Just like that?" she whispered, her voice a mixture of incredulity and hope.

"Just like that," he confirmed, shoving a couple more things into the bag and zipping it up. "Are you gonna be safe while you wait? Is Gray —?" He paused, the name tasting like ash on his tongue. "Is *Gray* going to be a problem?" he ground out.

"He'll probably sleep the whole time…and I'll stay right here, awake, where I can't…do anything."

He could practically feel her panic rising in her tight tone.

"You won't do anything wrong… You *wouldn't*. If you don't believe yourself, believe me. You may not know this, but I'm one of most highly trained and decorated naval officers around." He deliberately injected a cocky note into the grandiose statement, and it had the desired effect when she huffed out a reluctant laugh.

"I should be all right," she confirmed quietly, and the cold knot of tension that had formed in Mac's gut loosened just a little. It wouldn't fully loosen until he could see her in person, touch her, protect her.

"I'm on my way then, baby," he assured her. Just before the line went silent, he heard a soft *thank you* that felt like a benediction.

He was concentrating so hard on hauling ass that he almost didn't see Jenna, standing in the darkened kitchen and cradling a hot mug, until it was too late. The abrupt stop made him stumble a little on his prosthesis, and he cursed under his breath.

"Sorry, Jenna," he mumbled. His sister had always been nearly as much of a stickler about bad language as his mother was.

"You know, I find that it doesn't bother me as much anymore, in the grand scheme of things," she answered. When he looked at her face, a strange expression crossed it before he could identify it. Wistfulness? Sadness? "As long as you don't curse in front of Connor, mind you," she continued, sounding more like the prim and proper sibling he'd always known. "Heading out so soon?" she asked, gesturing toward his bag. Maybe it was just the light, but her eyes seemed suddenly very sad. Tired.

He gave a quick nod. "Urgent call. I'll come back, though, Little J." He used her childhood nickname. "Will you apologize to Connor for me?"

She gave a shaky nod, and Mac wished he could see his little sister better in the low light. There were several shadows on her arms and chest, and right across the bottom half of her face, making her almost look bruised.

"He'll be disappointed — he loves his Uncle Mac — but I'll make sure he understands."

Mac flashed her a semblance of his usual grin. "You're the best. You know that, right? Definitely my favorite younger sister."

"That's what you always tell me," Jenna answered. He thought her smile looked like it might have wobbled, but it was too dark to be sure, and his mind was already halfway to the airport. She set down her mug and gave him a quick hug. "Now, you take care, and text me when you get there."

"You don't even know where I'm goin'," Mac answered.

"No...but with the way you're practically jumping out of your skin to leave, I'm guessing it's Minnesota — and not to go to work, either."

"You always were a sharp one, Little J," he answered, smiling once more before he turned and stepped out of the kitchen door into the sultry night air.

Chapter Five

I'm coming right now. She held on to the words like a talisman as she held herself rigidly awake for the next few hours of the night, sitting on the floor of the hallway outside Gray's room. She longed to dart into the bedroom she'd claimed across the hall to grab a pillow to put under her butt, which was falling asleep. The carpet was thick, but not *that* thick. Still, remembering the horror she'd felt as she found the brooch that she still clutched into her fist so tightly that she knew it would leave marks, if not small punctures, kept her rooted in place. As long as she stayed sitting out here, she wouldn't miss anyone or anything — even for an instant — that might try to get into Gray's room, and she could hear everything.

Being alone with her thoughts wasn't very comfortable, though. She was heartened by Mac's willingness to immediately come to her, no questions asked, but at the same time, worry was like a lump of clay heavy in her gut. How could he trust her? What if she wasn't worthy of that trust? Most importantly, how could he still care so much?

Even though she'd thought she might never sleep again, she must have still drifted off since she started to dream of a huge, dark place. The air was so thick that she could barely see her hand in front of her face, but somehow, she knew that Gray was there with her.

"Gray? Is that you?" she called out, but the sound was muffled. Was it fog…or smoke?

"I'm scared, Lala. It's dark in here." Gray's voice sounded like it was far away, blocked by something, and her heart clenched in her chest.

"I'm coming, baby." Lana ached to find the little boy, to make everything better, but her body felt curiously heavy.

The sound of him coughing penetrated the mist that seemed to have filled her brain. *Oh, God, is the house on fire?* Even her alarm only registered dimly, though.

With muted horror, almost as if it were happening to someone else, she felt a cold touch on her bare leg, creeping higher. She froze, every fiber of her body seeming to close in on itself in rejection of the touch.

"*Laaaaah…naaaah.*" It was more of a ghostly whisper than a sound, but it gave her goosebumps. Lana desperately tried to force her eyes open, to move her arms or her legs, but no part of her body or brain seemed to want to cooperate.

"I don't like this!" Gray's voice was thin and reedy.

Something leaned close to her, and she heard the voice again. It was deeper this time, but so disembodied it could have been either male or female. It sounded practically demonic. "*Laaaaa-naaaah…you'll hurt him.*"

Lana opened her mouth, and finally some sort of hoarse croak emerged. It allowed her to shake off some of the stupor of her nightmare until she was able to hear a thudding sound, like someone heavy approaching.

Her throat was scratchy, and she began to cough, but she ignored it as she tried to wake up, driven by an overwhelming urgency. *But why?* Suddenly, she remembered. *I have to get to Gray.*

When she cracked her eyes open, the hallway was filled with smoke. Next to her, Gray's door was closed. The loud sound — definitely footsteps — was getting closer. She tried to stand but her limbs wouldn't hold, so she dragged herself to the door, turning to face whoever the attacker was. She was determined to put herself between Gray and anyone who might mean him harm, even if she was only able to trip the intruder.

She heard a strange hissing noise, followed by a man's cough. Before she could freak out at the confirmation that there was definitely a strange man in the house, the sound of his voice made her practically go weak with relief.

"Lana! Honey, where are you?" The voice was deep, frantic with worry, and unmistakably Mac's.

"Here," she tried to call, but it was just a scratchy whisper. Her throat was so dry it practically clicked when she tried to swallow. "Mac," she tried, and this time, a little bit of noise came out. It seemed to be all he needed.

Like a conquering warrior, Mac's huge form emerged from the haze. His expression was grim, and he had a fire extinguisher that she recognized from the kitchen pantry held comfortably in one hand. As she looked up, the smoke was starting to thin, so she could see how his expression transformed from stony to tender — so tender that she ached.

"Darlin'," he said in a hoarse voice. "I put out the fire in the kitchen, which looks like it started with the toaster, but there's too much smoke. We need to get you to where there's more fresh air."

As he bent to lift her, she answered urgently. "Gray! We need to get Gray."

"Lala! Are you coming?" The little boy's voice was high and terrified, and she heard a thump — probably his foot connecting with his door — behind and to her left.

Mac's eyes had narrowed when she'd mentioned Gray's name, but at the sound of the child's words understanding apparently dawned, and Mac gave her a terse nod. He twisted the doorknob, but it didn't move. She heard his low curse, then he caught and held her gaze meaningfully.

"Move back from the door, baby, okay?" she called as forcefully as she could. It hurt her throat to try to be loud, but whatever pain she felt was worth it to keep Gray safe and protected.

"'Kay, Lala," she heard in return, along with some rustling.

Mac must have been satisfied that the little boy had moved since he slammed his shoulder into the door. If he'd been a smaller, less-muscular man, the thick door probably wouldn't have budged. He was tall and broad-shouldered, though, and her brother had told her that Mac worked out for hours every single day. However grudgingly, the door gave way, leaving Mac charging into the room.

Somehow, Gray must have evaded Mac to come right out into the hallway, where she'd managed to struggle to her knees. As his small form rammed into her with a surprising amount of force, Lana felt herself go practically boneless with relief at how solid and unharmed his sturdy frame felt. She hugged him tightly, breathing in his post-bath little-boy soap smell. She didn't realize she was crying until Mac knelt down next to her, wiping a tear from her cheek.

"Let's get you both downstairs," he said, and she nodded shakily.

She stood, still holding Gray, and Mac put his arm around her to lend his support as she rose and as they limped down the hallway, which continued to clear of smoke. The air coming in from multiple open windows was cold, and she didn't think she'd felt anything more wonderful. It was quiet...much too quiet, in fact. The smoke and security alarms, which she thought were connected to each other, should have been blaring like crazy.

Pausing at the top of the stairs, Lana looked up at Mac. "Wait! How did you get in without the alarms going off?"

Mac grimaced. "Darlin', when I got here, the front door was wide open, and all the alarms were disabled."

At his words, Lana's expression grew horrified, then guilty — so guilty that he was surprised she didn't just collapse under the weight of it.

"Oh my God," she whispered hoarsely. "I was having a dream...but how could I have done this, even in my dream, and not remembered any of it?"

He didn't fully understand her meaning, but he didn't need to understand to know that she was blaming herself, just as she had been over the phone. He'd rushed here without stopping, but something had still obviously occurred in the interim. Whatever it was, Lana looked as if she were hanging on by a thread.

He settled her, along with the little boy, onto one of the couches in the more informal of the two living rooms he'd passed on his sprint upstairs. Lana immediately pulled the little boy into her lap, and he snuggled so close it looked like he would have burrowed into her if he could. For her part, she was whispering reassuring words and running her hands over him as if checking for any injuries. Mac expected she wouldn't find any, since Gray's room had appeared clear and pretty normal...apart from being locked, that was.

Without thinking, Mac tried to crouch in front of them, then toppled forward onto his knees, hard. He winced. The pain was almost worth it, though, when his startled grunt seemed to shake Lana out of her own thoughts. He stroked his hands along her forearms, which were soft and warm, and she focused on him.

"Are you all right?" she asked, her eyelashes fluttering downward. "I'm sorry... I should have asked that first."

He shook his head. "I'm fine...more worried about you. Are you guys okay?" Mac dug into his pocket for his cell. "I'll go ahead and call 9-1-1."

The choked sounds that both Lana and Gray made sounded nearly identical.

"Do you... Do you think it's absolutely necessary?" Lana's eyes were large and haunted. Mac noticed that Gray's lower lip and chin trembled before he pressed his head back into Lana's side.

"I, ah, I guess it might be okay if we don't call them...since I can see that you, well..." He cleared his throat. "That it's an unpopular suggestion," he finished lamely. The relief in Lana's eyes warmed him right down to his toes, and he vowed to do whatever was necessary to make her look at him like that again. He took her free hand — the one that wasn't stroking Gray's hair — mostly because he couldn't stop himself from touching her, reassuring himself she was all right.

"The next logical question, then, is what do you remember…?" He trailed off when he saw the sudden pain and guilt in her expression. Her tension practically vibrated from her hand into his arm where they touched, and Gray looked up worriedly as well, in spite of the sleepiness that crept into his eyes.

"Before we go over everything, though, darlin', I think I'd better secure all the doors and windows again, hm? Wanna tell me the security code in case I can get the system working?"

Her smile was tremulous but trusting. Good Lord, even scared and tired, Lana was so beautiful in the low light that she nearly took his breath away.

"Thanks, Mac… My gosh, it means…" Her voice was thick, and he thought he saw an extra shininess in her eyes before she lowered her gaze to the little boy. "It means so much to me," she finished, and told him the code.

He squeezed her hand. "Of course, Lana," he whispered, forcing himself to turn away before he said something he shouldn't — something she wouldn't welcome.

Mac started with the front door, clicking the deadbolt back into place. The security system seemed to be in perfect order, accepting the code Lana had given him without so much as an extra beep or chirp. It wasn't a new system but it was a good one, with small cameras inside and out. It was the kind of system that someone who liked privacy as well as protection would install. Mac wondered who owned the house and why the hell Lana was staying here, alone, with the little boy.

As he went room by room, checking the lock of every window and door, he noticed two things. First, the house was large and comfortable…nowhere near the size of the Fitzhugh family compound, but spacious, with luxurious touches like a home theater and even what looked like a basketball and bowling alley. Second, it was distinctly a family home, complete with a wall of family photos of a good-looking couple alone, then with baby and toddler Gray.

Mac felt a flare of uncomfortable jealousy at the idea that this might be Lana's boyfriend's home — that she could be with the man in all the pictures — but that man appeared deeply in love with the woman from the photos, some of which were quite recent, featuring Gray as well. One of them looked to have been taken at a VIP box at a hockey game that Mac had watched on TV just a month earlier. Mac knew Lana well enough to say with confidence that she'd *never* be someone's mistress. *Is she watching her friends' child? Why wouldn't she call* them?

He puzzled over the circumstances while his body protested at how hard he'd pushed it, especially his right leg, as he rushed around the strange house, but he wanted to ensure that every single point of egress was secured. It wasn't until he got to one of the last rooms to be checked — a classic sort of study and library — where a different picture caught his attention from the corner of his eye. It was of the woman who was obviously Gray's mother, but she was much younger. In the picture, she was sitting next to a pool with Lana, but it was Lana like he had never seen her. Sure, she was much younger, but that wasn't the biggest difference. No...this Lana, beaming out at him, appeared lighter and happier than he'd ever known her. Her face held an innocent promise, inviting him to share her joy.

He was suffused with a curious sadness, that he'd never seen that sort of openness in her expression. He'd assumed — and he, of all people, knew how foolish it was to assume — that she'd always been the polished, elegant, mostly reserved woman he'd gotten to know months earlier. Obviously, there was a hell of a lot more that he didn't know — and hadn't even tried to find out.

When he limped back into the sitting room, no longer able to even pretend his leg wasn't bothering him, Lana jolted, looking up at him owlishly. Gray was fast asleep at her side. He sank gratefully onto the empty cushion on her other side.

"House is secure, and nothin' besides the front door appears to have been touched. I had no problems reengaging the security system. Looks like there should be camera footage, though. We can review it in the mornin'." His voice was low and gravelly.

"I think it might already be morning," Lana answered with a tired smile, raising her eyebrows as she inclined her chin toward the large bay windows. Indeed, Mac saw the pink and orange hints of dawn.

"Well, after a few hours of sleep, then," he amended. "You and the kiddo look all tuckered out."

Lana grimaced. "Gee, thanks, Lieutenant Commander MacKenzie. A lady always loves to hear how haggard she looks. You're not exactly worthy of posing as Mr. July on the Navy pilot of the month calendar right now, either."

Her snippy tone surprised a laugh out of Mac, which he promptly stifled.

"I'm glad I amuse you," she continued, lifting up her stubborn chin in a gesture Mac had noticed she generally only used with her family...and him. She hadn't spoken to him like that in months, and he'd missed the hell out of it. A curious sort of relief made him feel lightheaded.

"I'd rather see your fire than your terror any day, darlin'," he answered, and all the fight went out of her. "Aw, honey, no...I didn't mean to make you go back there in your mind." He took her hand again and squeezed. All his protective instincts, barely leashed as they were, roared back with a vengeance when she leaned against him with a heavy sigh. "Wanna tell me what's goin' on?" he invited, trying for a light tone but unable to keep from sounding a little growly.

When she looked up at him, her expression was curiously intent, as if she were committing every line of his face to memory. He quirked up one eyebrow questioningly.

Her dry laugh was sad. "Just...just looking before you realize I might not be someone you should care much about."

The sadness in her voice was breaking his heart. "Why don't you tell me and let me be the judge, hm?"

Chapter Six

Soaking up the last of Mac's approval before his expression transformed as she knew it would — as she'd seen it change in others before on the few occasions she'd mustered the courage to tell them the ugly truth of her past — Lana took a deep breath, steeling herself for the same sort of reaction. As she'd drowsed while he checked the house, she'd realized what a disservice she'd done to him five months earlier, letting him leave while knowing he'd taken her comment about him being a certain kind of man as an insult, when instead she'd meant it as a statement of fact that he was too good for her. He was gracious and honorable enough to forgive her and help her anyway, but she owed him the truth as to what sort of woman he'd agreed to help. *Well*, she mentally amended, *as much of the truth as I can handle telling him now.*

"I'm not sure where to start," she began, not hedging but honestly too fuzzy from the night's events, along with the stress of the past week, to put together a coherent thought.

"Start wherever you'd like, sugar, and I'll follow," Mac answered, stroking his fingers along her bare forearm in a caress she wasn't sure he was aware he was giving her. Goosebumps rose on her skin.

"Is this Gray's house?" he prompted gently, inclining his chin toward the sleeping little boy.

"That's right," she murmured. "You must not have heard, but a little over two weeks ago, my childhood best friend and her husband were killed in a car accident, and I became Gray's guardian." She couldn't help the thickness in her throat from the tears she fought, but she forced herself to continue. "Luckily, because of stories Sam told him about me, he thinks of me as a sort of auntie, but I thought it would be even harder for Gray to move to a new home and lose every one of his familiar surroundings, so I moved in here right away."

Mac's voice was a low rumble in the quiet of the early morning. "Makes sense. Very kind and thoughtful of you, although I would expect nothing else."

Even after the tension between us, Mac thinks I'm kind and thoughtful? Lana felt a warm sense of belonging rise inside her, unbidden, and some of her tension relaxed, if only slightly.

Silence stretched between them until Mac spoke again. "You said that Gray's mom was your childhood best friend. Were you not still friends?"

The twist of guilt and shame inside of Lana's chest was so familiar that it barely registered anymore. "We...had been estranged for a long while, but once upon a time, we were as close as sisters." Lana thought of her own brothers and how difficult it could sometimes be between them. "Maybe closer, because we chose our friendship. We shared everything back then — dreams, secrets, promises."

Mac nodded slowly, and a beam of pinkish light filtered into the room, hitting his face so that it highlighted his green eyes, making them glow like emeralds. "I get that. But if you weren't in touch, why — ?"

"Why did Sam and Cain name me guardian?" It was something that Lana had asked herself countless times over the past two weeks, and she kept returning to the same conclusion, although she was almost afraid to believe it. "I, ah, don't know if I'll ever be certain, but…in spite of the way I betrayed — no, *ruined* — our friendship, I want to think that Sam knew that I meant my promises to her." Lana swallowed around the lump that had formed in her throat. "Maybe…maybe she was able to forgive me."

Mac stilled, and when she dared a glance up at him, he looked more thoughtful than horrified.

"What happened?" he asked in a quiet voice.

The familiar shame and guilt over her own selfishness made her cheeks heat and her throat tighten, more than it had in years. She just couldn't tell him — not yet, maybe not ever. Mac probably deserved to know, but she wasn't sure she could bear it if he looked at her with the same disappointment that she still saw flashes of sometimes in her brothers' eyes, even after all these years. *And they don't even know the full truth*, the nasty voice in the back of her mind that sounded suspiciously like her mother reminded her. *And now you might be hurting the precious little boy Sam entrusted you with, too.*

"Can't... Can't..." The words were hard to get out as she was suddenly breathless, as though she couldn't suck enough air into her lungs. She waved her hand in front of her, almost as if to physically push the memories away.

She expected Mac's anger or frustration, but she should have known better. Instead, she could feel his body relax next to hers, as though it were unconsciously trying to guide hers, and he stroked one large hand, so warm that she felt it through her thick sleep shirt, up and down her spine in a gesture that was all comfort.

"It's okay, sugar. You don't have to tell me anything about the past you aren't comfortable with. It won't change a thing." His voice was low and soothing, everything she needed. If she could have gotten enough oxygen, she would have gasped a thank-you, but instead she concentrated on slowing her racing pulse.

Still, as she calmed and the all-consuming panic receded, another powerful emotion pushed itself forward, twisting her stomach—worry, mixed with dread and self-doubt. "Maybe they shouldn't have trusted me, though," she forced herself to confess.

Mac didn't stop the long, comforting strokes on her back.

"You said somethin' like that before. Wanna tell me why?" he prompted.

In as objective a tone as possible, Lana recounted all the recent incidents from the past few days, forcing herself to relive them almost as a bystander, even though it made everything inside of her cringe. As she spoke, she became more and more convinced of her own guilt.

"I don't understand how or why, but I think I must be somehow causing all these accidents...making them happen, even subconsciously..." She trailed off miserably, increasingly certain that it was the best thing for everyone if she followed up with a psychiatrist, immediately. "Tonight, I even thought I heard a voice...but it was almost as if it came from inside my head. It's like it was my own conscience, warning me of how dangerous I'm becoming for Gray." She shivered at the memory.

"Where's the brooch now?" Mac asked. She'd been so wrapped up in her own recollections that his question almost startled her.

"Uh..." She looked down at her hand, still slightly scratched from where she'd gripped the piece of jewelry before. "I suppose I must have dropped it." A horrible thought occurred to her. "Oh my God, Mac. Did I even really find the brooch?" she blurted out before she could stop herself.

"Don't go there, honey," he answered in his usual slow, measured tones. She could almost hate him for being able to sound so charming without even trying. Maybe she'd try to be angry with him about it...later. "Were you holdin' it with this hand?" he guessed.

She gave him a terse nod.

All rational thought fled as he lifted the hand she'd been examining. He studied it, tracing the small cuts on her palm before placing a soft kiss right in the middle that made her stomach flutter.

"These small cuts are in a distinct shape. You didn't imagine this," he said. His expression changed, growing harder than she'd previously seen it. She had a flash of intuition that maybe this was his work face. She knew he'd been a very respected Navy pilot and medic before he'd been forced by his injury to retire. "I'm not sure you imagined anything," he continued, "but if it will make you feel safer, I'll act just like I would if you were truly doin' these things subconsciously. That way, we'll get to the bottom of things with you and Gray safe and sound." He curved his lips into a wry smile. "Assumin' that you trust *me* not to be behind everything, either?"

The faith he demonstrated in her — the confidence, even after she'd pushed him away — made something within her chest that she hadn't realized had grown so tight loosen considerably.

"I trust you," she whispered, feeling her eyes sting with grateful tears. *Mac doesn't think I'm crazy*, she thought. *He believes me... He believes me.* She let her head lean against the hard plane of his pectoral muscle, breathing in his distinctive scent that made her feel safe.

His low murmur was so quiet she barely heard it. "You rest, darlin', and I'll watch over the two of you."

She only meant to close her eyes for a moment, but when she opened them again, she could tell from the quality of the light coming through the high windows that it must be daytime — mid- or even late-morning, probably — and overcast. She lay stretched on the couch, with a sleeping Gray still sprawled next to and half-on-top of her. A soft throw blanket covered them both.

Her first thought was worry that she might have somehow had another one of the strange episodes, and she stiffened, darting her gaze around the room. Cool relief flooded her as she saw Mac, seated nearby in one of the velvet-covered armchairs.

"Mornin', sugar," he said, as lightly as if it were completely normal for them to wake up together in the family room. "Before you ask, I've been near you for the past few hours and all you and Gray have done is sleep. Man, you both must have been tuckered out from more than just last night. I've been sittin' here for so long, though, that I might just be willin' to eat a cockroach if you offered me some coffee or a bathroom break."

He looked so serious that Lana couldn't help her laugh, surprising herself. When Mac's expression grew rueful, though, she realized he hadn't been joking.

"Oh my God, you're serious? You haven't even gone to the bathroom?"

Mac shrugged. "You were so worried last night, and I promised to watch over you. You're not the only one who keeps your promises." He raised one eyebrow. "It isn't the first time I've been trapped in place on assignment overnight, although this terrain is certainly different. View's much nicer, if I'm bein' honest."

The generosity that Mac had shown her was enormous, both by rushing to her, no questions asked, in the middle of the night, then by keeping watch so she and Gray could sleep, even making light of the whole thing. The affection that she'd started to feel from the first moment she'd met him returned and grew, like a living thing, warming her all over.

"Mac," she whispered, her voice hoarse with emotion. He caught and held her gaze, and something indefinable passed between them — something that made her heart speed.

The spell was broken, though, by a firm knock on the front door. She shot to a sitting position, earning a sleepy protest from Gray, and drew her eyebrows together.

"I wonder who that is," she said, speaking her thoughts out loud. "It can't be Mrs. Schultz. She only went on leave five days ago, and she said she needed at least two weeks away to take care of her husband. None of the other daily staff are scheduled today." Her heart felt as if it leapt into her throat at another horrifying possibility. "Shoot, I hope it's not the press. They've been leaving us alone so far, at least at home — since they got their pictures at the burial — but I know I can't expect that truce to last forever." She raised a hand to her hair, which was almost certainly a golden rat's nest at this point.

Mac looked both mysterious and sheepish. "Pretty sure it's for me. I probably should have asked first, but I sent some messages while you slept — calling in favors from service buddies, some contacts from the veterans' organization."

Lana made a sound of dismay. "Oh, no…these things have a way of getting around, and the last thing we want is the press to get ahold of this type of story."

He rubbed the back of his neck uncomfortably. "I, ah, may have let them know it was urgent." Now he met her eyes head on, his look unwavering. "Which, by the way, I believe it is. Honey, if you're not the one doin' these things — and I truly don't know, but I suspect you very well might not be — then someone has been comin' into the house with you and Gray at home, while you were cookin', bathin', sleepin'…"

The implication was as horrifying as it was clear. "Oh," she answered, her hand flying to cover her mouth. She'd been so focused on the horror of realizing that she might be more than forgetful, but the idea of this being a deliberate act by someone else, farfetched as it seemed, was even worse.

Mac rose, straightening his clothes, and she couldn't help but notice how tall and strong he looked, as though he were ready to stand between her and anything.

How could I ever push this incredible man away from me? she thought, her throat tightening with emotion. Then she remembered why, and she firmed her resolve again. *How could I not, when he deserves so much better than what I have to offer?*

He seemed to mistake her silence for ongoing hesitation, continuing to explain. "There's always a slight chance, but I really don't think any of these guys would let anything slip to the press. Loyalty runs deep, and even if it weren't me askin', word has gone around about what Fitz — and you — have done for veterans' groups. Even if some cameraman happens to be staking out your house right now, all he or she will see is a work crew. It wouldn't be that unusual for you to have security or other remodelin' work done, would it?"

Lana forced herself to refocus on what he was saying, and it made sense. She shook her head slowly. "No…that sort of work is not unusual. I mean, it would be pretty tasteless to be doing a renovation right now, but…we can spin it if we need to. Drew has a good agency on retainer, and we can just give them a heads-up. He and my grandfather — and Roger, of course — weren't happy when I told them I was going to rely on the security system at the house, but I just didn't want any disruption for Gray."

"You're all right with it, then?" he asked. She was touched that, in spite of his outwardly high-handed attitude, he truly seemed to care. She was used to men taking one look at her face and body, hearing her name, and immediately discounting her as ornamental.

"Yes, you have my full approval," she agreed. "In fact, given what's been going on, you have my go-ahead for other changes, too — whatever you think we need." She stifled a shiver at the idea of someone sneaking around for days on end without her noticing. "Gray's safety is paramount, and I can deal with any fall-out to make sure it's on me and doesn't even come close to affecting him."

The knock came again on the front door, not exactly forceful but also not patient.

"Thanks," Mac replied, inclining his head in acknowledgment. "I truly am sorry I didn't have the chance to ask first though, sugar," he added before going to the door and admitting a small group of tall, incredibly fit-looking men with military-short hair, the leader of whom gave Mac a hearty slap on the back.

"Nice house." The admiration in Gunderson's voice was clear. Mac tensed when he followed his old buddy's line of sight over to Lana rather than the structure.

"She's not on the upgrade list for today." Mac tried for an easy tone, but he knew he must have failed by the way Gunderson's chin snapped up as he examined Lana and Gray with renewed curiosity.

"Understood. Didn't realize that's how it was."

Good old Gun, never uses ten words when five will do. Mac smiled to himself at the recollection of how a rumor on his ship that the huge new sailor from Minnesota couldn't speak at all had begun circulating at one point until Mac had nipped that shit in the bud.

Gun had found out, and he'd inadvertently earned himself a loyal friend.

"What's on the list, then?"

Gun's question pulled Mac out of his memories. He shook his head to refocus himself.

"First and foremost, security. Need a new system ASAP," Mac said.

His former fellow officer looked every inch the contractor as he nodded, but while Mac had every confidence that his friend was solid at all aspects of construction, he knew something that Gunderson would never publicize. The man was a genius with security, and he had an awesome team, mostly comprised of other former military brothers and sisters. More importantly, Gun was discreet to the point of coming off as surly to almost everyone.

"We don't just need the new system, although that's priority one. We want a full analysis of the footage and logs of all activities."

Gunderson inclined his head in acknowledgment. "Timeframe?"

Mac thought about what Lana had told him about when things had seemed to escalate. "Start about five days back, but go further if we don't find anything."

"Gotcha," Gun confirmed. His blond hair was so pale it was almost whitish, even his beard, which rustled slightly as he nodded again. "Might take time, but we'll hustle."

It was a lot to ask of Gunderson's crew, to drop everything. In fact, as Mac scanned the forms of the men still arriving, he realized that either Gunderson's crew had increased exponentially or there were a lot of extras.

"You bring some extra day laborers, Gun?" he asked.

Gun curved his lips up into a slight smile. Instead of making him look more innocent, though, his expression grew more determined...grimmer, even. Mac was forcibly reminded of the mood he'd always felt just before heading into a hot zone. It was a mix of nerves, resolve and undeniable excitement. "Couldn't keep 'em away when they heard...and you were so vague, I thought you might have some other stuff that needed doing."

Stepping closer, Mac spoke more quietly. "You thought right. I want every inch of this place searched and secured, including the grounds."

"Happy to take the grand tour." Gun deadpanned. "What will you and Ms. Fitzhugh be doing?"

Something about the inflection in Gun's voice when he said Lana's name made Mac look at him askance.

Gun shrugged. "C'mon, man. You can't grow up anywhere between Fargo and Chicago and not be a little in awe of the Fitzhughs."

Mac had known that Lana's family was famous, but now he realized how much she'd downplayed the level of fame and attention she must have always known. *Maybe why she doesn't want to settle for a man like you*, a nasty voice whispered in the back of his mind. He ignored it in favor of the task at hand, something he'd had to become really adept at during his long recovery.

"Well, whatever else she is, she's also the little sister of a Marine brother." Mac thought he'd spoken the words in an even—if dispassionate—tone.

Gun's beard shook with the force of a stifled snort. "Yeah, sure...*that's* what you see when you look at her." He huffed what might have been a low laugh.

"It's because her brother is a Marine that you texted me at oh-five-hundred this morning. I would never tell another shipmate what to believe, but man, your story's better than the fairytale I read my baby niece last week."

Mac's first impulse was to argue but...Gun wasn't wrong. He sighed. "Ms. Fitzhugh and I will be taking Gray out somewhere to distract him, but I'm hoping someone can follow behind us."

"You know we will," Gun confirmed, narrowing his eyes. "But if something's making you this nervous, why don't you want to take regular security? Surely, she has some from her own detail?"

"She told me when we met that she doesn't keep her own detail. She doesn't like it. As for bringing on anyone new, we just really don't know what's going on, so it makes sense to go real easy at first...plus, I know that she would worry about disrupting the kid's life even more," Mac answered.

Gunderson nodded thoughtfully, sympathy flashing across his expression. "I heard about the accident on the news...tragic."

"Horrible," Mac agreed. "And entirely unexpected."

Gun's curiosity was obvious, but he didn't ask anything further. "All right, then. We'll be fast and quiet...but someone will stay on you."

Mac clapped him on the back, feeling like he was hitting a solid slab of granite. "This really means a lot, Gun."

"Any time, Doc," he answered, using the nickname Mac had as a medic. "Even if I hated your fucking guts—which I don't—I wouldn't have made it out of that last op alive without you. None of us would have. All you ever have to do is ask."

"You don't owe me anything...not a thing, *ever*. I just did what I had to—what anyone would have, in the same spot." Mac firmly believed that.

Gun's smile was barely discernable under his full, bushy beard. "We know we don't owe you. Just happy to help a brother out," he confirmed, looking at something over Mac's shoulder.

Before even turning his head, Mac knew by the indescribable scent that teased his nose—the one he'd never quite been able to forget, that tormented him with memories every night just before he fell asleep—that it would be Lana.

Chapter Seven

Lana hadn't intended to eavesdrop on Mac and the extremely tall stranger with the Viking-like appearance and unmistakable military bearing. Still, she wasn't going to pretend that she hadn't heard anything.

"You saved all the men here?" she asked, the question slipping out before she could reconsider.

The parade of emotions across Mac's face might have been comical in another context. First he looked stony, then embarrassed, until his expression finally slid into one of resignation. "When you're a pilot and a medic, saving people comes with the territory," he answered gruffly. "I was doing my duty."

Placing her hand on the hard, bunched muscles of his upper arm, she took a step closer. While all the new arrivals in the large room seemed to now be moving around with a purpose, they also appeared to be avoiding looking at Mac and her. *Interesting. Wonder what he told them about me...about Gray. Watch out for the kid since the lady might be slightly deranged?* She dismissed the thought as unworthy of Mac. He was probably just uneasy about accepting compliments or praise. She was desperately curious to know more, but that didn't mean she should press him to find out.

"I didn't mean to make you uncomfortable. That's incredible, Mac," she answered gently.

He didn't say it, but the way the harsh lines around his eyes and mouth slightly softened told her he appreciated her words.

"Where'd Gray get off to? One of the guys take him?" Mac asked, pointedly changing the subject.

Lana smiled wryly, and Mac raised a questioning eyebrow. In an overbright voice, she said, "Oh, *where* could Gray have *gone*? I wonder *where* he could *be*!"

She heard and felt muffled laughter behind her where the little boy clung to her leg. He didn't seem to want to be more than a couple of inches away from her this morning, and she couldn't blame him. Mac immediately caught on to what she was doing.

"I can't *imagine* where he could have *gone*! I'd better look for him. It's like he just *disappeared*!" He answered, matching her over-the-top intonation.

As expected, Gray jumped out in a fit of giggles, his whole body shaking with them. "I'm *here*! I'm *right here*!" he crowed triumphantly. "I was behind Lala, but you couldn't *see* me!"

Lana couldn't stop the matching grin that she knew must be plastering her own face. In the short time they had spent together, Gray had experienced a great deal of sadness, but he was still so full of joy that it rolled off him in waves. She knelt down next to him without thinking, wanting to be closer to eye-level with him, then was nearly knocked over as the little boy threw his arms around her and squeezed.

"*Oof,*" she said laughingly, ruffling his copper-colored mop of curls, so like Sam's. "Gray, I want to officially introduce you to my friend. His name is Mac."

"I already know who he is," Gray informed her confidently.

Her chin nearly snapped as she looked up at Mac, shocked. Her heart went back to its normal rhythm, though, when he appeared as puzzled as she was.

"You *do*?" she asked.

Gray nodded vigorously. "Oh, yes. He's the fireman from last night. He picked you up. Don' you 'member, Lala? Firemen are cool."

Mac's rich chuckle was like warm honey, sweet and comforting. "Good memory, kiddo. I was there last night, but I'm not a fireman. I am a retired Navy medic, though."

Looking thoughtful, Gray shoved two fingers in his mouth so that his words were slightly garbled when he continued.

"Is that like being a fireman? I love firemen. My mommy and daddy took me to see the firetruck once, and I got to sit in it an' everything. I love dogs, too. Firemen have dogs."

Lana loved that Mac seemed to be truly listening to the little boy, following the twists as Gray spoke.

"Well, it's not the same thing, but I would call them similar. Firemen are often the first people on scene when something bad happens, and they provide first aid—that's medical help—so I would say that firemen and medics are on the same team."

Gray took his fingers from his mouth and narrowed his eyes. "Do you have a dog?" he asked.

Lana couldn't help her snort of laughter at how suspicious Gray sounded, and she thought she heard Mac make a similar sound above her.

"Well, buddy, I haven't been able to stay in one place for long enough to have a dog of my own for a while now, but I can confirm that I love dogs and hope to have one again soon. How's that?"

Mac was such a natural with Gray that it made Lana remember the deep affection she'd heard in his voice when he'd spoken of his nieces and nephews. He must be an awesome uncle, and he'd probably be an even better father. The thought made the ever-present knot of shame and regret in her gut tighten until she nearly winced from it.

Tilting his head to one side, Gray looked so serious that she reached out to squeeze his shoulder.

"That makes sense," he answered. "Okay. You can stay with us."

Mac quirked one side of his mouth up into a half-smile that was devastatingly attractive. "Great," he answered. "Now that that's settled, I thought maybe we could get out of the way of everyone here and head to the zoo or the mall."

Lana drew her eyebrows together and frowned. "Are you sure that's wise? With, uh...well, everything?" Her mind raced as she imagined what could happen if she somehow forgot to do something for Gray while they were out in public. It would be even worse if someone were filming her.

Holding out his hand to help her up, Mac lifted his broad shoulders into a slight shrug. "The way I figure it, everything has seemed centered here at the house. I'll be watching over both of you, wherever we go, and maybe it'll do us all some good to put some distance between us and this place…so we can come home to a fresh start." The way that his green gaze held Lana's felt significant.

"I like monkeys," Gray said.

Lana hid another smile at how much of a non sequitur his statement was, but of course, in his mind, it was probably just logical. Someone mentioned the zoo, and he liked monkeys.

"I suppose we can head to the zoo, then, but maybe Gray and I can wear hats and sunglasses?" She made the statement a question, but she could tell from Mac's expression that he understood.

"Oh, I like the sound of that. I'll be out with a couple of regular spy-types. Cool. I'm only sorry I forgot to pack my fake mustache stash."

Lana shot him a grateful look. *Why did I wait so long to see him again?* she asked herself for about the hundredth time. *Oh, right, because he's way too good for me, and it's wrong to take advantage of him this way. Yep. That's right.*

Looking at Gray's face—a bit pinched and drawn from the events of the night before—shining now with a new hope and happiness, she couldn't be sorry for calling Mac. She only hoped he would forgive her.

With Mac's help, she and Gray were both ready in no time. It felt easy, as if they'd been working together for years, and wasn't *that* a thought that she needed to stay as far away from as possible? Before she knew it, they were dressed, packed and standing in the circular driveway. Mac's friends had considerately parked their multiple work vans all to one side, so that Mac and she had plenty of room to leave. She'd seen him exchange a sort of subtle nod with the Viking guy again, along with another younger-looking man who appeared to have followed them outside, but at a respectful distance. *Like a guard?*

Mac's watchful gaze was at odds with his easy manner with Gray.

"Are we ready to see some monkeys?" Mac asked encouragingly.

"Yes, please," Gray answered, suddenly shy as he hovered near her leg.

Lana had to stifle a smile at the preschooler's appearance. It made something in the region of her heart twist, to see him attired from head to toe in the classic preppy style Sam had always favored, so that he looked like he was headed out for a day on a sailboat. Of course, she looked a bit odd as well, wearing a bulky cable-knit turtleneck, along with a ballcap and large sunglasses. She just hoped the outfits bought them some peace from the local press. She thought they had a good chance, as long as no intrepid reporter happened to be at the zoo with their family today.

"Do you want me to drive?" Lana offered, and her stomach sank when Mac stiffened, his easy manner cooling noticeably.

"I'm still more than capable of driving a car, plane, anything—you name it." He answered. If the daggers he'd shot from his eyes had been real, she would have been lying in a bloody heap on the ground.

Her cheeks grew hot with embarrassment. No, it was more than embarrassment. *Shame...*that she'd made him uncomfortable. She tore off her sunglasses so he could see her expression.

"That's... I'm so sorry, Mac. That isn't what I meant at all." She held his gaze, willing him to understand and believe her. "I just thought that, because I know the way to the zoo already and we should take my car since that's where Gray's car seat is…it might be easier," she finished lamely.

His manner was still stiff, but Mac did her the courtesy of seeming to truly consider her words. His aquiline nostrils flared, and his chest visibly rose and fell twice before he answered.

"I'm… I can admit I'm still touchy about my leg. Sorry, sugar." His smile was more of a grimace, but she appreciated the attempt. "I'd prefer to drive, if it's all the same to you. I promise I can use a GPS the same as the next man — probably better, in fact — and I like the idea of being in control…just in case."

He didn't finish the sentence — *in case of what?* — but she thought she understood. It was terrible enough thinking that she might be the one causing all the strange occurrences. However, if his theory was correct and someone else might be behind them, might follow them, observe them… Put that way, Lana would be more comfortable with Mac driving, too.

The little boy remained silent, but his head ping-ponged between the two of them, betraying how closely he was following their exchange. Lana was glad they'd managed to keep their words mostly vague.

"Of course. Here are the keys," she answered, forcing a casual smile for Gray's sake, even though her hands trembled a bit as she handed them over. Mac covered her suddenly cold fingers with his own. They felt warm and strong, hardened from work.

"This outing — public and spontaneous — should be just what we need, and we'll come home to a nice, *safe* house."

Mac's voice was smooth and confident, utterly calm, but she understood what he wasn't saying. The upgrades he was arranging might be extremely important to their safety, and it would be better if they weren't around, in order to let the crew work freely.

He leaned in closer, nearly brushing the wisps of hair near her ear, and said something so low it was obviously meant only for her. "I'll watch out for you, darlin', and that's a promise."

He pulled back so quickly that she could have imagined the words, but his level stare made her pulse flutter so that she fumbled as she pushed her sunglasses back on, nearly poking her eye out in the process.

"Gray, baby, let's get you in your seat, okay?" she managed to squeak out.

Mac's lips twitched with amusement, but he remained silent as he crossed around to the driver's side, leaving her to help Gray with the variety of straps and clips.

* * * *

It wasn't too far to the zoo, but when Mac darted a look at the rearview mirror, he saw that the little boy had conked out so hard that his head lolled to one side.

"Looks like Gray is out cold," he mused, and Lana swiveled her head around to look at the small, sleeping form.

"Poor little guy... He's probably still tired from not sleeping well for the past few nights. He's been having so many nightmares..." Lana blanched as she trailed off. "Oh my God, what if none of them have been nightmares? I feel like an awful guardian—and a horrible person—for not believing him."

She sounded so agonized that Mac couldn't help but reach over to pat her leg, covered only by her thin leggings. "Kids have nightmares, especially kids who have recently experienced something traumatic. How could you have known?" he reassured her.

She shook her head, and he smiled again at the stubborn jut of her chin. People often mistook Lana Fitzhugh's outward beauty and serene manner for complacence, but really, she was anything but. The fire she kept tightly leashed inside of her burned so bright that he was surprised she didn't just explode sometimes from the force of it.

Of course, fire or not, it was normal that she was worried now by what was happening. She had good cause. Mac's honest sense was that she wasn't the origin of the accidents, but he owed it to both of them — Lana and Gray — to keep an open mind and explore the possibility that it could be Lana herself who was causing them, remote though he felt that possibility was.

"I should have known...should have *seen*," she insisted. "He was terrified, genuinely terrorized, at night...kept saying there was a man in his room." She shivered visibly. "How absolutely horrifying that there really might have been someone there and I just ignored it...or maybe I was standing there myself and just can't remember."

Mac squeezed her leg and Lana covered his hand with hers in a gesture that seemed unconscious.

"Sugar, I'm not saying this just to make you feel better, but I truly think I would have done the same thing. If my nephew woke up crying, I would tell him he had a bad dream and leave the room after I got him back to sleep. There's no shame in assuming something is a horse until you have proof that it's a zebra...or hell, an okapi."

Her smile was tiny, but genuine. "Thank you, Mac. Really. For being there, and answering...coming right away, saving us, calling your friends... I can't tell you how grateful I am."

Mac swallowed whatever emotion that threatened to rise in his throat, which he frankly didn't want to examine too closely.

"Made you a promise," he answered gruffly.

"And you kept it," she answered, her tone an odd mixture of tenderness and resignation.

"Not that I'm not completely honored that you trusted me enough to reach out to me — I told you that you always could — but am I allowed to ask why you didn't want to call your brothers or your grandfather?"

Because his hand was still on her leg, he felt the sudden tension in Lana's frame.

"My grandfather hasn't been well, and Drew and Fitz are both away. I already told you that, I believe."

Mac loved the little snippy bite to her tone. Sweet, Lana was spectacular. Feisty, she was nothing short of glorious. He fought the urge to squirm in his seat at the sudden tightness in the region of his groin, which was totally inappropriate at the moment. He also couldn't have stopped his attraction for any reason. He knew. He'd tried.

"You did tell me that, sugar, but I just don't believe that's the entire story of it."

"That's awfully presumptuous of you," Lana huffed, and he gave in to the urge to shift to make room for his growing arousal. What was it about her attitude that got to him like nothing else?

"Acknowledged. I find that I'm a presumptuous sort of man when it comes to you. Am I wrong, then?" he asked.

The silence in the cabin of her SUV stretched until he thought she was just going to ignore the question. Her reply, when it came, was so quiet he almost missed it.

"You're not wrong," she answered.

Mac waited, unwilling to push further than he had already.

"They don't trust me," she started, then interrupted herself. "No, that's not right. They *do* trust me. *Now*. A little bit. But they didn't, for a long time...and I had to work really hard to earn their trust back. I think...I just can't stand the idea of losing their respect for a second time."

Her statement was charged in so many different ways, Mac wasn't sure about where best to start. Just as he opened his mouth, the automated voice of the GPS rang out.

"In point-five miles, take ramp right at exit number forty-two."

Gray made a low murmur in the backseat, and Lana half-turned to look at the little boy, making reassuring noises as he returned to full wakefulness. Mac reluctantly pulled his hand away from her leg, and their moment alone was officially over.

As they got off the highway, following the signs, Lana surprised him.

"Since I answered yours, can I ask you a question in return?" she asked.

Mac felt his eyebrows shoot up almost to his hairline. "Of course. Anything...or, almost anything, given present company," he qualified with a slow smile.

"What the heck is an okapi?"

His guffaw rang out loud in the small space, and Gray giggled, too.

"Hm, now, this just proves how sorely you need a trip to the zoo, Miss Fitzhugh. I bet Gray knows the answer." He tilted his chin up toward the rearview mirror, and Gray, now fully awake and appearing like he was practically bouncing with the knowledge, was happy to comply.

"An okapi is an animal from Africa, with a front like a giraffe and a bum" —Gray interrupted himself with a chortle at his own description of that body part —"like a zebra." He looked at Lana seriously. "They're on my favorite cartoon."

Lana's expression grew suitably impressed, and Mac's heart warmed at the unexpectedly tender moment. It felt...*right*, like they were a family, even if only for a short time.

Chapter Eight

Lana felt close to Mac today, as if the intervening months of missing him had never happened. Even though she knew how dangerous it was and how unfair to him if she led him on, she couldn't seem to help herself, especially when he smiled. Mac smiled a lot around Gray and even more around her. As they walked from exhibit to exhibit at the zoo, in spite of the circumstances that had led them there, it felt like a bubble outside of real life, and she laughed so much her cheeks and stomach ached in the best way.

It was a cool, drizzly spring day, and Lana thought that the weather, in addition to the fact that it was a weekday, might have kept most would-be visitors away. It was so quiet, in fact, that they might have thought they had the place to themselves a few times. Mac was endlessly patient with Gray, listening to whatever the preschooler had to say with real interest and picking him up several times to get a better view of certain elusive animals.

For his part, Gray showed more enthusiasm than she'd seen from him the past few days. Sure, he'd had fun when they'd ventured back a couple of times to the playground, but now he seemed to be responding well to being away from the house for a longer time. Lana wondered if it had more difficult for him than she'd imagined, being surrounded by all the memories of his parents. She was no expert, and discussing it with a child psychologist hadn't made her one, but she did understand that children — especially small children — processed grief very differently from adults.

When they reached a fork in the walkway that would either take them back to the buildings or on the longer path to Minnesota-centric animals, she paused to look at Mac questioningly. He'd been unobtrusively checking his phone at regular intervals. Even though his easy manner didn't change, something about the set of his mouth and chin told her that there was something he'd read that he didn't like.

"Any preference on the road less traveled, here?" she asked, raising one eyebrow as she motioned toward the more wilderness-looking path. It truly did seem darker, almost rustic in comparison to the wide, bright sidewalk back to the buildings.

"Oh, darlin', I should warn you right now that I will always choose the longer way. It's not a character flaw so much as a personality trait," Mac returned, sliding his phone back into his pocket with a mischievous grin. It was infectious.

"Is that a fact? What if it's much harder and likely to have obstacles?" she prompted.

He stepped closer, so that she could smell the distinct, spicy scent of his skin. She fought the urge to breathe more deeply, to imprint it into her memory forever.

"I always enjoy taking my time, and a few obstacles don't scare me one bit." His look was intent as he spoke, and she knew without a doubt they weren't only speaking about the walkway — or any walkway, for that matter. Her skin felt suddenly shivery and sensitive, with goosebumps prickling on her arms.

"Cold?" Mac asked, tracing his finger along the little strip of skin between her ear and her baseball cap. His eyes were dark with concern and…something else.

Lana shook her head jerkily, mesmerized by everything about him. She longed for nothing more than to lean into his touch. "Not cold," she whispered.

Just when they drew together like two magnets, unable to resist the pull of their attraction, Gray's high voice piped up between them.

"Yay! Wanna see the moose!" he enthused, skipping off lightly down the darker, longer path.

Heat flashed instantly to Lana's cheeks, this time from a mixture of embarrassment and frustration. She wasn't sure which was more prevalent. "I guess we'd better…um…" she gestured lamely toward Gray's back, his lead on them growing.

Mac's half-smile was both amused and rueful. "I guess we'd better," he agreed.

They followed Gray in silence for a while, and Lana couldn't help but notice the beauty of their surroundings. "This really does look just like the north woods of Minnesota. They did a great job with this area," she observed, remembering a long-ago class trip.

"Do you have a lot of wilderness experience? A secret passion for hiking, maybe, that you've been hiding since you were a kid?" Mac teased.

His words, joking as they had been, stung more than they should have. Nobody in her family would ever have taken her into anything remotely resembling wilderness when she'd been younger, much as she'd begged. Now she didn't have any friends close enough to even consider asking someone to go hiking with her. Certainly, none of the smiling acquaintances she saw regularly at galas, openings, and museums would be appropriate to ask on a rustic outing. Her brother and Clara had met in the wilds of northern Minnesota, but that was a separate piece of their life, just for the two of them.

"Hey now," Mac said in a low voice, sidling closer. "I didn't mean to make you sad, sugar. Just having a hard time picturing you in the forest."

Lana sighed and gave a small shrug. "I certainly haven't gone often," she acknowledged. "We did go on a school camping trip once, though. Sam was my tent-mate, and we had so much fun. We ate our weight in charred s'mores and hot dogs." She chuckled at the memory. She'd scarcely ever felt so stuffed, and it had totally been worth it.

"Sounds like the perfect trip," Mac commented, and she noticed that they'd come to stop in front of the railing of an exhibit with a giant moose sign.

She nodded thoughtfully, remembering. "Oh, it was...well, *mostly*. One of the days, it was kind of misting for hours and we got soaked, so we hung all our clothes from the top of the tent to dry overnight and slept in our underwear. Then, in the middle of the night, I woke up to feel something cold and wet on the back of my neck...which turned out to be a giant toad!"

"I know this story," Gray piped up excitedly. When had he skipped back toward them?

"You *do*?" Lana asked, astonished.

He nodded his head vigorously, making his little plaid hat slip to a rakish angle. "Oh yes! Mommy told me she picked up that slimy, giant toad-beast and it went pee-pee all over you!" His peal of laughter made the dreary day seem suddenly brighter, and Lana couldn't help a deep answering belly-laugh at the memory.

"That is *exactly* what happened... Oh my gosh, we couldn't stop cracking up! After she, uh, escorted the toad out and we zipped the tent fully closed, that is!" Lana could practically see it all again in her mind's eye and feel her stomach clench with helpless mirth. She and Sam had had tears streaming down their cheeks with the absurdity of it.

Mac's expression was soft as he looked at her, curiously tender. "I would like very much to have seen that," he murmured, and she swatted his shoulder playfully.

"Well, there isn't likely to be a repeat performance!" she answered laughingly. She was distracted from their conversation by Gray's whoop of excitement.

"Oh, look! Here comes a moose!" he shouted, practically dancing with excitement.

As Lana looked, a huge form was indeed lumbering toward them. The sheer size of the creature was amazing, and she sucked in an unintentionally loud breath.

"Don't worry, Lala," Gray said, patting her side, most likely because that was what he could reach. "Moose are big, but gentle. They're my mommy's favorite." He went suddenly quiet, and his face lost all traces of excitement as he curled his hand tightly into Lana's sweater.

"You okay, sweetie?" she asked in her gentlest voice, taking in the sudden pallor of Gray's cheeks, which had been pink just the moment before.

"I wanna go home," he answered, his gaze riveted to the moose even as his lower lip trembled. "I wanna go home *now*."

Lana exchanged a brief look with Mac, who reached down to put his massive hand on the little boy's shoulder. Her throat felt suddenly thick with tears.

"Sure, buddy. We can leave now...no problem," Mac said in a light, normal tone, and they headed for the exit.

* * * *

Gray was asleep in his car seat before they even left the parking lot, which his experience with his nieces and nephews told Mac was pretty normal after an exciting outing like going to the zoo. Plus, the poor little guy was probably emotionally drained. Damn, Mac was feeling a little tender himself. Lana turned worried blue eyes on him, though.

"Is he okay? Is that normal...for him to sleep so hard and so fast?" she asked, her genuine concern obvious.

"Oh yeah... A few years ago, when I went the aquarium with my oldest nephew, he was talkin' one minute, then sat down on a bench and fell asleep from one word to the next." Mac still chuckled at the memory. Ethan hadn't even trailed off. Just *bam*! And the words had stopped. "I had to carry him out of there, and he slept the whole ride home. When he woke up, he was his normal, crazy self, and my sister — my older sister, who knows everything about everything — told me it was absolutely fine, so it must be true."

Lana's lips twitched with amusement, and he fought the completely irrational urge to lean over and kiss them, right then and there.

"You always sound so affectionate when you talk about your sisters." Lana's astute observation took him by surprise, but it shouldn't have. She was thoughtful. "You must love them very much... I'm so sorry I took you away from a visit with them."

He half-turned, as much as safe driving would allow, as he answered. "They are indeed two of my very favorite people. Our daddy died when I was a teenager, and it was real hard on our momma, so Kim—that's my older sister—had to deal with a lot from Jenna and me, even more after our momma passed as well. But you better believe that my sisters were the first two to write, call and visit me in the hospital." He kept his attention on the road, but half of his mind went back to those dark days, lying there feeling like he might have woken only half a man, and realizing what a jerk he'd been to hurt and drive away so many people in the past, including his young fiancée.

He cleared his throat, wondering why the hell he'd blurted out so much. He scarcely ever mentioned his recovery to civilians, and here he was blabbing his head off. "But I'm not sorry you took me away from Jenna's house, because you needed me." He spoke in a low voice, but he meant every word.

"You're such a good man—" Lana started, but Mac cut her off before she could say more.

"I get it, darlin'. I'm a good man, but I'm not your sort of man." He tried not to let the bitterness that he'd attempted not to stew in—not too much, anyway—over the past few months seep into his tone.

He was startled by the warmth of her hand on his bare forearm where he'd pushed up the sleeves of his sweater after they got back into the warm SUV.

"That's *not* what I was going to say," she answered, and something about her words or the inflection of them made stubborn hope, heretofore just a tiny little green shoot, start to unfurl like a seedling in his chest. It wasn't blooming, but it could.

Before he could ask what she *had* meant, then, a loud chirp from the Bluetooth system made them both jump.

"What was that?" Lana asked, their easy camaraderie gone as she worried her lower lip with her teeth.

"Nothin' too bad, sugar," he reassured her. "I linked my phone to your system and rigged it to make the emergency alert sound if a message came through from Gun. It just means I somehow missed something from him."

When she didn't move to press anything, Mac was surprised. When the possible solution dawned on him, he knew he was right.

"Oh my stars, could it be that Miss Lana Fitzhugh, with her fancy, top-of-the line, Bluetooth-compatible navigation and stereo system, doesn't know how to use it?"

He could practically feel the vibrations of her irritation in the molecules of air between them.

"I'm sure I could figure it out," she started, sounding like she'd been sucking a lemon. "But I never answer the phone in the car. It isn't safe!"

Her tone was so schoolmarmish — although what a sexy schoolmarm she would be, and that was a fact — that he nearly laughed. Like before, though, his cock hardened almost painfully, and his laugh came out instead as more of a strangled groan. "Oh, darlin'...you're killin' me."

She sniffed, the very picture of moral superiority — like a librarian righteously shushing him — and he almost hated to burst her bubble, but then again...

"It's not unsafe if you link it up to your own system. Not illegal, either. But if you're so concerned, maybe you could allow me to keep my full attention on the road while you push the 'play message' button on the touchscreen?" He thought he'd sounded magnanimous, but he realized he must have overdone it by the heat of her glare. Still, she pushed the button. When they heard Gun's message, they both sobered.

"Man, you must be really out of range because your phone isn't sending messages through, ringing straight to voicemail. Hope you appreciate this. You know I hate talking on the damn phone. We're all finished here — more extra guys showed up, just wanting to help out. Everything's good, but all the security footage from the past five days has been erased, backups and all."

Shit. Mac felt a twist of unease, deep in his gut. He'd suspected it had to be something like that, but he'd hoped he was dealing with an amateur and they could just put an end to things right now. Instead, it sounded like they were going to have to put some more work into finding who was behind everything.

"Looks like some pro-level work," Gun's message continued, confirming what Mac's instincts had told him. "Doubt your lovely Lana would be able to get that deep, but I've been surprised before. All points of egress are secured with the new system, coded to your prints. We're taking off within fifteen or so. You should remember to add your woman as soon as you get back. Text me if you need anything — and Mac, I mean that."

There was a fumbling click — Gun really did hate talking, so it was a testament to their friendship that the other man had left such a long message — and the car was quiet again. Mac's ears heated at the words his friend had used to describe Lana. *Lovely. Your woman.* Gun wasn't far off base, but Mac knew how uncomfortable it might make Lana. He should have known that wasn't the part of the message that concerned her, though.

"So, we still don't know if it was me," Lana said in a small voice.

Mac took the exit that would bring them back to the affluent suburban neighborhood where Gray's house was. In spite of the cool day, the trees had buds on them, and everything felt poised to burst into springtime.

"Well, no…not for certain, but Lana, I really don't think you're the one behind any of this," Mac answered.

Her sigh was heavy. "I just…thought we'd know. But now I still have to wonder."

"Well, darlin', how good are you at deleting security footage and hacking into security system mainframes?" he drawled, trying to lighten the mood but also half serious.

She shrugged. "I… Well, I'm the kind of woman who doesn't link up her phone to Bluetooth, but I can't help but feel that this is somehow still my fault."

They pulled into the long, round driveway in front of the house. True to what Gun had promised, it was now empty of all other vehicles apart from the Jeep Mac had arrived in, the one he kept at the airport when he was away.

"Honey, maybe someday you'll trust me enough to tell me why you're so determined to believe the worst about yourself, because I have to confess that I don't see a reason—not a single one—when I look at you."

Lana's answering huff of laughter was wry, and self-deprecating. "There's a reason...a lot of them. Trust me."

"Agreed, on one condition," he answered, and she looked up at him questioningly. "I'll trust you," he explained, "but only on one condition."

It was so quiet in the enclosed space of the vehicle that he could hear the faint swish of the wind through the trees.

"Seems fair," she finally answered.

He felt satisfaction roar through him at this sign of bending, no matter how small.

"I'll trust you if you trust me," he replied simply.

Her smile was a beautiful thing, for all that it was small. "Mac, I already do. You have no idea how much."

Chapter Nine

Mac wasted no time in arming the security system, after programming in Lana's fingerprints as well. She had started to protest, but he'd made the completely reasonable point that he didn't want her — or her *with* Gray — accidentally locked out for any reason. He also pointed out that if she were programmed as a user, the new system should not only film any of her activity but also record her specific access being used. As they sat in the kitchen that night, Mac playing blocks with Gray at the kitchen table while she cooked a simple, preschooler-friendly meal, she had to admit that having the house searched and new system installed had made her feel worlds better. More reassuring than that, though, was Mac's steady presence.

The kitchen had trendy recessed lighting, which gave a warm glow, but the fatigue on Mac's face was unmistakable in the little lines around his eyes and mouth as she surreptitiously observed him from where she stood at the gas stovetop. *And he* should *be tired. The poor man was up all night flying, then watching over you, before you and Gray dragged him all around the zoo,* her inner voice scolded her. The well of sympathy in her chest didn't surprise her, but the impulse, nearly impossible to resist, to walk over and smooth her hands over the crinkles in his forehead did. *Bad, Lana, bad... Hands off,* she reminded herself again.

"Somethin' sure smells tasty, doesn't it, Gray?" Mac observed, drawing the little boy in easily. She'd initially been surprised by how quickly they'd bonded, since Gray had been so unsettled lately, but of course she shouldn't have been. Mac's charm was irresistible. She ought to know.

"Mm-m, yummy," Gray agreed, only briefly looking up from the tower he was building. He jutted his tongue out of his mouth and to one side in concentration, and the gesture looked familiar. Her eyes grew misty when she realized that it was something that his father, Cain, used to do when he sketched. Cain had always carried a sketchbook around school with him. Lana only wished she'd known him better, so that she could have had more memories to tell Gray about.

"Chicken stir-fry. Sorry that it's nothing fancy." She directed that last part of comment toward Mac. "It'll be ready soon. Gray, baby, is it okay if we move your tower over to the play rug?"

"Okay, Lala," Gray agreed easily, and she was grateful she'd caught him at a good listening moment. He seemed to vacillate between listening pretty well and utterly ignoring her.

Mac lifted the entire structure easily in his large hands. "Buddy, I'll take the tower itself if you can put the rest of the blocks in the bucket and carry those?"

Watching Mac's tall, strong form as he carried the unstable structure so carefully, with Gray following trustingly behind him, made her feel warm and melty inside. She wished, more than anything, that she could be worthy of such a man, but it had never been more apparent to her that she wasn't. Mac was born to be a father, and he'd be a spectacular one.

Gray took his time arranging the bucket just so, and Mac returned to the kitchen before the little boy did, coming up behind her and stealing a piece of green pepper from the pan. Her entire body thrilled at his nearness, although she had to laugh at how he fanned his mouth after popping the vegetable into it.

"Hot, hot, hot," he repeated, and she felt her cheeks stretch again into a silly grin.

"Food tends to get that way when you cook something," she chided, but she couldn't bring herself to sound too stern.

"Oh, darlin', if you knew how much I love it when you get all straitlaced on me, it would make you blush." His words were a mere rumble of sound, close to her ear, barely audible over the sound of the food sizzling, but true to his prediction, she felt her cheeks flame.

"You shouldn't talk like that in front of Gray," she scolded.

He raised one eyebrow, and his emerald gaze practically sparkled. "There's no way he can hear me from all the way over there," Mac countered.

He was right and she knew it, but she refused to concede. "Dinner's ready!" she bellowed, virtually into Mac's face, and his bark of laughter was highly amused.

"Message received loud and clear, sugar," he said dryly, and she was so pleased with herself that she almost missed what followed. "I'll keep those sorts of comments for when we're alone."

She practically sputtered with indignation, then caught herself. That was exactly what Mac wanted, and she wouldn't give in to the impulse. "Can you and Gray set the table while I dish up?" she asked with a sweet calm that she didn't feel.

The saucy tilt of Mac's lips told her he didn't feel it, either, but he nodded easily enough. "Of course. You're the boss, and we're your humble servants. Isn't that right, Gray?"

"Oh yes!" Gray nodded enthusiastically. "I want to play servants." He paused, looking thoughtful. "What's a servant?"

Mac and Lana both burst out laughing, and Mac leaned down to ruffle the little boy's shiny copper-penny hair.

"A servant is someone whose job it is to take care of someone else, but it's a bit of an old-fashioned term, now, I think," Lana explained, as Mac went about setting the table. The steam from the stir-fry warmed her face and one curl, heavy from the moisture, escaped her haphazard hairstyle and flopped over her right eye. If any of the society matrons she regularly had brunches and afternoon teas with could see her now, they'd be mortified on her behalf.

Gray was silent, obviously considering. Then, his smile blazed. "Okay, then! You're my servant, Lala, and I'm yours!"

Lana had to smile again. The way she'd explained it, it made total sense.

When Gray spoke again, it was softer. "Mac, too?" he asked, and Lana's heart clenched with her own form of longing.

She forced a bright expression and made a non-committal noise as they carried the plates to the huge, dark-wood kitchen table.

＊ ＊ ＊

"That was amazin', Lana," Mac said appreciatively, leaning back in his chair and rubbing his flat stomach.

The pink flush that stained her cheeks made her look even more vibrant and pretty. She shook her head. "Oh, it was nothing much," she answered.

He'd noticed the same thing when they'd gotten to be friends months before…that she wanted to divert all attention and praise from herself.

"Maybe not to you, sugar, but I'm not a great cook myself, and you can only imagine some of the sh—" He darted a glance at Gray before correcting himself. "Uh, *slop* that they served in the service. I mean, sometimes it was awesome, but out in the field…" He shuddered theatrically. "Chicken, fresh veggies and delicious sauce, all cooked by someone other than me…? That sounds like a gourmet feast in my book."

"You can have my peppers," Gray offered helpfully. He had eaten most of the meal—actually, a pretty hearty helping for such a little guy—but he had pushed all the green and yellow peppers to one side of his plate.

"Mighty generous of you, Gray, but I think I'm full. Did you have something to say to Lana about this meal, though?" he prompted, then worried that perhaps he'd overstepped. He had just been trying to treat the little boy the same way he would treat one of his nieces or nephews, but he realized Lana might not appreciate it. He'd seen her with her own family a few times. While she and Fitz were building back up to something that resembled a more typical sibling relationship, she had seemed pretty formal with her grandfather and oldest brother, Drew.

"Thank you for cooking, Lala," Gray answered obligingly, his little-boy voice high and sweet. Lana's pleasure at the thanks was clearly written in her expression, and he thought maybe he hadn't erred after all. "Can I go play blocks some more?" Gray asked, but he nearly didn't get the question out before his face broke into a huge yawn, so large that Mac thought he heard his jaws crack.

"You can play tomorrow," Lana answered. "You need to have your bath and get ready for bed soon."

Mac raised himself from the table, grabbing his and Gray's plates as he headed toward the sink. His right leg protested the movement, burning so much that he had to stifle a flinch when his full weight landed on the socket of his prosthesis. It was always worse once he'd been sitting down for a while if he'd recently been really active. He worked out hard, every day, but they had done a lot of walking at the zoo, and his leg wasn't thanking him. For a second, he felt the familiar anger that had been his constant companion when he'd first woken up in the hospital to find he was missing his foot and most of his calf, but he forced himself to take deep breaths and to think of what he did have. *A strong body,* he reminded himself, *with a top-of-the-line prosthesis.*

"Are you okay?" Lana asked quietly. "Does…does your leg hurt?" she continued, haltingly, as if worried she'd offend him.

He forced one of his easy smiles, all charm, even as he wanted to grit his teeth. The last thing he wanted was for Lana to start to pity him. *No fucking way.*

"I'll be fine," he answered, but he thought his words might have more of an edge than he'd intended. "Why don't you and Gray head on upstairs, and I'll take care of these dishes, hm?"

"I don't mind —" she started, but he cut her off firmly.

"No, no...you cooked, I'll clean. Them's the rules. I don't make 'em. I just live by 'em." He thought his joking tone must have been more successful this time when her lips curved into a small smile.

"If you're sure?" she checked again.

"Absolutely. I'll be up in a flash," he confirmed. He made short work of the dishes, forcing himself to compartmentalize the discomfort of his leg. With an angry grunt, he allowed himself to pop two ibuprofen into his mouth, which he generally avoided. He needed to be in top form, though. As he walked over to check the security system, simultaneously logging into the monitoring app on his phone, he turned the day's events over in his head...both what they'd learned, and what they hadn't.

Something messed-up was going on here. Of that much, he was absolutely certain. Sleep deprivation and stress could cause a lot of different reactions, and there were ways to make someone believe something that wasn't true, so even if the origin of these issues ended up being Lana — a possibility he still felt was pretty remote — he knew, down deep into the very marrow of his bones, that she wasn't doing anything deliberately. However, the camera feeds being erased pointed much more toward an outside actor or actors.

But still, was this person or people acting alone, or trying to physically and psychologically manipulate Lana? More importantly, why the hell would someone do that? What would it gain them to have Gray hurt and Lana believe she was to blame? The attacks, because that's what they seemed to be—*attacks*—appeared directed at Gray, with Lana set to question herself. They'd had potential to seriously injure the little boy, but they didn't truly feel like attempts on his life. Or, if they were, they were extremely roundabout. He needed more intel, and he needed to keep his eyes peeled for anything that seemed remotely off.

When he'd confirmed that everything looked good with the system—no attempts at access, house fully secured—he flipped to his messages and saw one from the analyst on Gun's team. It was a report on threats to the Fitzhughs, and he skimmed it on his phone. At a glance, most of the hate was directed at Lana's oldest brother, Drew, and her grandfather, Pat, which made sense. They were both public figureheads of the company and the family. The section of the report on Fitz, Lana's middle brother, was tiny in comparison, which also seemed reasonable, since he'd been in the Marine Corps, distanced from his family name and history, until very recently. When Mac reached the section on Lana, it was only of medium length, but it was by far the most disturbing.

He forced himself to fight the impulse to storm upstairs. She trusted him, and he had to trust her…even when he was furious at her for keeping something so significant from him—maybe *especially* then.

When he reached the landing for the second floor, he heard an outsize splash and walked in to find a damp-looking Lana drying a wet and squirming Gray, flushed from his bath, with an enormous, plush towel that looked softer than he'd ever seen, even at a hotel. Not that he frequented five-star hotels or anything, but since working for Pat Fitzhugh, he'd seem some posh places, and his sisters both kept some bathroom accessories that were 'For Guests Only'. He teased Jenna about it mercilessly.

"All clean?" he asked, congratulating himself on how normal he sounded.

"Yep!" Gray confirmed happily. "Lala let me play with *two* duckies, 'cause I was so helpful." He held up two fingers around the towel, which Lana was vigorously patting him with.

"Is that right? That's great, buddy," Mac answered.

"Can I take them to bed with me, Lala?" Gray asked, and Mac saw that he was still clutching two small, yellow rubber ducks to his skinny little chest.

Her hair was fuzzy and mussed — very unlike her usual, sleek hairstyles — and her face looked pink and shiny from exertion. Mac thought he'd never seen Lana look so beautiful as she smiled indulgently. "Well now, only if you keep being helpful as I get you into your jammies, then into bed."

Gray's face scrunched like he was going to protest, but he looked down again at the ducks and thought the better of it. "Okay, okay." He heaved a sigh as though he were enormously put-upon, and Mac turned his chuckle to a snort.

He followed the pair, watching Lana get Gray ready from the doorway of the little boy's room. When he turned to leave, to give them more quiet time, Gray's voice stopped him. "Stay, Mac. Come tuck me in, too," he murmured sleepily. Mac couldn't have resisted if he'd tried, so he didn't and sat down next to Lana on the side of the bed.

The room smelled like baby powder and tear-free soap, but Lana herself exuded her usual light, mysterious perfume, along with just a hint of sweat. Mac had to force a decidedly un-bedtime-friendly image from his mind of other ways he could help her work up a sweat.

"Will you sing again, Lala?" the preschooler pleaded. The look Lana turned on him was uncomfortable, as if she weren't pleased to have herself revealed this way.

"Don't hold back on my account," Mac encouraged, and he was truly curious. This was a whole different side of Lana, and he liked it. He liked it very much.

"Okay, then. Just a short one, though," Lana agreed, and Gray beamed up at her.

Lana's speaking voice was lovely. Mac had already known that, having practically hung on her every word when they'd been planning the gala together all those months before. He thought maybe he'd heard her hum once, too, in a low, sweet soprano. Nothing — *nothing* — could have prepared him for her singing voice, though. She was like a freaking cartoon princess, charming birds right out of the trees. The song she chose was one he only vaguely recognized, something old-fashioned, but the casual beauty of her voice, simultaneously rich like honey and clear like a goddamn bell, was unmistakable. When she'd finished, Gray was asleep, and Mac was struck dumb with admiration.

The silence lengthened, and Lana shifted awkwardly. "I think Gray's asleep," she observed. When Mac still didn't answer, she nudged him with her leg. "Gosh, was it that terrible? You told me to go ahead, and Gray seems to like it."

"That was glorious, darlin'… You sing like an angel, and that's not even a mild exaggeration." He stroked her cheek, unable to keep himself from touching her, any part of her. Her breath hitched in her throat.

"Uh, thank you?" she answered, sounding so unsure of whether he was lying that it made something inside him ache.

"It's the truth, nothing more or less," he answered, beetling his eyebrows and feeling thunderous all over again as he recalled the other truth that had carried him up the stairs. "I could talk about your singin' all night, but we need to talk about somethin' else more urgent. Is there a good place for us to speak, where we won't wake him up?" Mac lowered his voice to just above a whisper, suddenly conscious that he should be quieter for the little boy.

"He generally sleeps pretty heavily, unless he's having one of his nightmares," Lana answered, and he could tell she was hedging slightly. "But we can talk in my room. It has a sitting area and it's close, so we'll hear him if he makes any noise. What do you want to talk about?" she finished warily.

He shook his head stiffly, and she seemed to understand that he wanted to wait. Only when they were settled onto the green-velvet button chairs in the corner of her room did he speak again.

"So, the good news is that the new security system is working well, and there haven't been any unknown attempts at entry recorded, nor have we seen anything concerning on the footage since the new camera network went up this afternoon."

She nodded, letting out a breath so that her chest fell visibly under her soft-looking sweater. "That *is* good news," she answered. "Why do I sense there's bad news, too?"

He pursed his lips, feeling the same exasperation he'd felt when he read the report...mingled with real fear for Lana.

"Not bad...just, Gun's guys have been working on gatherin' intel, and the first report they sent was a preliminary collection of threats to your family."

"But everything that has happened at the house has centered around Gray, hasn't it?" she asked.

"Overtly, yes," Mac agreed. "But this is all definitely about you, too, at least somewhat. Even if that weren't the case, though, I would want to cover all our bases."

"I guess that makes sense," Lana conceded. She'd turned on just one side lamp, and her hair looked like spun gold in the low light, but her eyes were shadowed, making it impossible for him to fully read her expression.

"Lana, why didn't you tell me you've had so many stalkers?" he asked bluntly.

She stiffened and looked away. "Nothing serious. And it comes with the territory of being a Fitzhugh. I didn't think—I *still* don't think—there could be a connection."

"The report said that one of them broke into the apartment you used to keep downtown and destroyed some of your things. Is that why you moved fully back into the main house with your brother and grandfather? Because of this deranged fan?" Mac tried to keep his tone even, but *shit*, this was scary stuff. Psychologically, stalkers were a breed apart. They might look and act mild most of the time, but when they fixated, it was nearly impossible to truly escape them.

"If you call him a fan, it makes it sound like I put myself out there...like I *perform* somehow, which I definitely don't." She bit her lip. "But yes, I guess he was sort of a fan. He met me at a charity event, then began following me. And the, um, incident was part of the reason I gave up my apartment and moved home, yes."

She looked so lost, so alone, that he reached over without conscious intent, covering her entwined hands with his. Her fingers were cold, and he felt her tremble.

"Honey, that is some crazy, scary stuff to have happen to you," he said gently, all his anger fading in the face of her defeated posture.

She blew out another breath and offered him a tremulous smile. It was her weakest attempt at the expression he'd ever seen.

"I think it happens to every famous person. It's the price we pay for the lives we have," she reasoned, but Mac shook his head.

"No, no…darlin', that's not right. You bein' born to a wealthy, well-known family doesn't mean that some wacko gets to invade your space — your private, sacred space — and chase you out of your home. You don't owe that to anyone."

When Lana finally met his eyes, hers were shiny. "You're so sweet, Mac, but I don't think most people would agree with you. And you shouldn't be so quick to absolve me. You don't know what I deserve."

Again, Mac felt it, just out of reach, fluttering at the edges of his understanding. There was something she wasn't telling him, that he wasn't getting, and it was important.

"Did you tell your older brother? Or your grandfather?" he asked, but he was almost certain he knew her answer.

She pursed her lips. "There was no need to bother them. They have their own issues with the press, their own histories."

I just bet they do, he thought, but he forced himself not to get too upset with the other men. They hadn't known, after all.

Mac wanted to push harder, but when he looked at Lana again, really looked, he saw that she was worn out to the bone. Her face, always pale, had grown nearly white, and deep purplish smudges had appeared under her eyes.

"I just... I want to *protect* you, Lana." Well, he really wanted to wrap her up in a quilt and hold her, and Gray, until all possible danger passed, but he knew that wasn't realistic. "To do that, you have to tell me everything. We're goin' in blind here, and I'm honestly not sure what might end up bein' important. We promised to trust each other earlier — or did you forget?"

She held his gaze with more of her usual spirit. "I haven't forgotten. Only...it's just something I live with, you know?" She shrugged, and it made his gut clench with sympathy. "The stalkers, admirers, possible danger...? They're always out there, and I just try not to think about it too much. I really didn't even factor it in as a consideration."

He understood, but it was a sad sort of understanding. She might need him more than she'd realized.

"All right. Well, as long as we're on the same page." He settled for squeezing her hands one more time, even though he really wanted to haul her into his lap and hold her the way she deserved. "I'm gonna turn in. I'm just next door, right?"

"You sure are," she answered. "Next to me and kitty-corner from Gray."

Mac had put his things down in his room earlier, but only briefly. He nodded. "Okay then, darlin'. You don't hesitate to call out if anything so much as feels off. I'm a light sleeper, thanks to the Navy, so I'll most likely wake up if I hear even a scratch that seems out of place. You and Gray can just catch up on all that sleep you missed out on."

"Thank you," she said softly as he left the room. He couldn't be sure, but he thought there was an undertone of sheer relief, and it warmed him to the core.

Chapter Ten

Mac hadn't been kidding about being a light sleeper. It truly was a skill he'd acquired — or rather, been forced to acquire — in the Navy. He'd had to both be ready to sleep at a moment's notice — because he never knew when he might get the chance again — and be ever-watchful. Starting at the Academy, almost anyone could wake him up at any time and expect him to function fully in that instant. It had only gotten worse when he'd gone out on missions. When he was flying, in particular, his reflexes had to be lightning-fast.

He didn't think he'd been asleep much longer than two hours when a soft cry of distress rent the air, stifled shortly. He pulled on his prosthesis as fast as he ever had, cursing every millisecond that it took, but he'd drilled himself enough that the motions were fast and practiced and he was headed over to Lana's room almost before he knew it.

When he stumbled in, she was huddled on the floor, her eyes as wide as saucers. A little bit of moonlight filtered in through the window, and she appeared almost frozen in horror. He slowed his movements, the same way that he would with a wild animal.

"Lana, honey, did you hear somethin'? See somethin'?" he asked gently, having an instant of unease that maybe she wasn't really awake or cognizant of him. Then he heard a low, hissing voice.

"*Laaaaah-naaaah.*" It sounded nearly, but not quite, like the wind itself, neither masculine nor feminine. "*Youuuuu'll huuuurt hiiiiiiim,*" it continued.

Lana made a broken sound and covered her ears, turning wild eyes toward him. Anguished.

"Do you hear it? Can *you* hear that?" she asked in a hoarse voice, sounding almost afraid of his answer.

"I sure as hell do, clear as day," Mac confirmed, rage like a living, breathing thing in his chest. *Who the fuck put some sort of recording out to scare a woman who was taking care of an orphaned preschooler?*

He grabbed her phone, where he'd installed the same security-monitoring app earlier as he had on his, and checked all the feeds, which were clear. Next, he disabled the security just on the two windows closest to her bed.

While holding the penlight from his bedside table with his teeth, he groped around and found what he was looking for underneath the first window. He held it up with a low cry of triumph.

"Wh-what is that?" Lana asked, her voice still thick with either tears or horror. He took the fact that she was speaking at all as a good sign, though.

"It looks like a simple device but diabolical. A plain old playback device on a timer. I'm guessing the guys didn't find it when they swept the house because it's not receiving or transmitting anything. 'Dead', we would call it. Someone mounted this bad boy under your windowsill, and I figure they likely set it to go off only when you're sleeping."

"Why would someone do that?" she asked, shifting enough so she could kneel back on her heels. She wore soft-looking shorts and a tank top, and her hair was mussed so that it went everywhere.

Mac considered the question as he shut the window, rearming the security alarms via her phone before placing it back on the nightstand. "I can't think of any reasons other than to either mess with you subliminally when you're asleep or to terrorize you if you happen to be awake…like how it happened tonight." He sat down on her bed, turning the device over and over in his hands.

"I feel like an idiot for not thinking to search where you did — outside the window. For assuming that…well, you know…" She trailed off, looking away.

"If we hadn't both heard it, and that thing had been saying *my* name…darlin', I would have been questionin' my own sanity, too," he admitted. "It sounded so much like the wind talking."

She turned back toward him, her expression surprised. "Thanks for saying that, even if it isn't true," she answered.

"I wouldn't lie to you," he replied simply, but it was an honest statement. "I learned my lesson, and I swore to myself that I wouldn't be dishonest again to the people I care about, not if I can help it." He blamed the intimacy of the setting, alone in the dark, for his sudden confession, but he found he didn't want to take the words back.

"Thank you," Lana repeated, and this time the words were laden with a deeper meaning. She opened her mouth as if to say more, but a shiver racked her body and she rubbed at her shoulders, curling herself into a ball with her knees tucked up under her chin.

Any thought other than concern for her fled. "Are you cold, honey?"

"Y-y-yes," she managed to answer, through clacking teeth. "And my heart...is pounding," she finished breathlessly.

Mac guessed she might be having a delayed reaction to her terror. "Why don't we get you back into bed, hm?" he said in an even, coaxing tone. He stood and bent at the waist, holding out his hands to her.

Her movements looked almost painful as she uncurled her arms, but his heart soared when she allowed him to help her up. Her skin was covered in goosebumps, and he put his arm around her to guide her back under the covers.

He pulled the mounds of comforters — *how many did one woman need?* — up over her, but when he would have turned, if not to leave, then to give her some space, she stopped him with a chilly hand on his forearm.

"Mac? Could you... Would you mind lying down with me?" Her voice was barely more than a thread of sound, but he felt her question in his gut.

"Of course, sugar. *Of course,* I wouldn't mind. It would be my very great pleasure, in fact."

Before he started to climb in next to her, though, she huffed in a sharp breath, as if she'd thought of something urgent.

"You want me to go check on Gray?" he guessed, and she looked shocked.

"How did you know?" she whispered, wondering.

His smile was a ghost of his usual grin. "Because you're a wonderful guardian auntie to him already, and I would feel better, too, knowin' he's okay. I reckon I'll be back before you can even count to ten."

He did his slightly lopsided jog across the hall, peeking into Gray's room. Mac stood there long enough to see and hear that the little boy was fast asleep, breathing evenly, with his two little rubber duckies still clutched to his chest, before Mac returned to Lana's room. He almost pulled the door shut, but then deliberately left it open so they could hear any noise Gray might make. And anyway, Mac figured it would also be a mighty leap to assume that Lana wanted anything other than his body heat in her bed.

"You're slow. I made it to twenty," she answered, looking like all dark eyes and light hair in her giant cloud of blankets. He liked that she felt up to ribbing him at all, though.

"Sorry... I couldn't stop myself from listening to his breathing," he admitted. "He's sleeping peacefully."

Her expression grew darker, somehow. Maybe wistful?

"You're such a kind man," she commented.

"I think a lot of people might disagree with you, ma'am, but I don't mind it one bit that you think so," he answered. He noticed the way she held the blankets to herself so tightly. "Are you still chilly, darlin'?" he asked, giving her the chance to tell him no.

She looked at him for a long moment, one that stretched and breathed. The light might be low, but he could still make out her thoughtful expression, the unmistakable flashes of need and yearning.

"Yes," she finally breathed, and it sounded like a confession. "*So* cold." Wordlessly, she lifted the covers, and he slid in next to her.

Lana knew it was wrong to use him this way. She might hate herself in the morning. *No, who am I kidding?* that persistent little truthful voice in the back of her head forced her to admit. *I will never regret any time I have spent with Mac MacKenzie.*

Mac curled his warm, strong body around her. "Oh, darlin', you're like an ice cube," he commented, rubbing her arms with his warm, rough hands. Every part of him felt muscular, and toasty — so deliciously cozy that she just wanted to revel in his heat.

"It's like my insides are frozen," she admitted, realizing it was an accurate description. Ever since she'd discovered that she might truly be the cause of Gray's accidents, it was as if a huge boulder of ice had lodged where her internal organs should be, numbing her from the inside out.

"For survival situations, we're taught to share body heat…skin to skin," Mac rumbled. It shouldn't have been, but it was one of the sexiest things anyone had ever said to her, and she felt her nipples harden where they were pressed against his chest.

"Skin to skin," she echoed. "Yes…we could do that," she whispered. Again, she knew it was wrong to lead him on this way, when she would still have to pull away from him, release him to give him the chance to find someone better, but would it be so bad to take this moment for themselves? "Maybe…could you try just taking off your shirt?"

"We can do this however you want to, darlin'," he spoke in his distinctive, sexy drawl, and she shuddered against him. He seemingly mistook the movement for cold and hummed with concern, quickly pulling his thin T-shirt over his head and throwing it…somewhere. She didn't care where. She didn't care about anything other than the expanse of tanned skin he revealed, dusted with golden hairs that were all she could make out in the low light.

She plastered herself to his chest so fast that he chuckled, the sound a low hum against her cheek. Still, he was so hot — like a human space-heater covered with muscles and smelling masculine and spicy — that she sighed with sheer pleasure and relief.

"Mm-m," she moaned, wrapping her arms around his waist. "So toasty." Indeed, the heat of his body seemed to radiate right through her thin pajamas and into her skin and muscles, starting to melt the icy knot of fear that had filled her.

"Better?" he asked, the question teasing.

"So much better," she agreed, squirming against him to find the most comfortable position and making a low sound in the back of her throat that she was embarrassed to admit sounded suspiciously like a purr.

Mac groaned underneath her, so that she felt the vibrations all along the side of her body that was pressed against his. "Honey, I'm doing my best here, but I'm not made of stone." His voice came out strangled.

"Are you... Is this arousing you?" She blurted the question before she could consider how ridiculous it sounded. *Of course* that's what he was talking about, and she'd revealed more about her relative lack of experience with men than she'd intended.

"More than you know, Lana." He gave a dark puff of laughter. "I've been dreamin' about lyin' with you like this since the first moment I met you... No, maybe even the first moment I saw you, across the office, before your brother even introduced us."

She raised her head to look at him, and his eyes gleamed like fathomless pools in the dim moonlight filtering in through the windows. She was reminded forcibly of how he'd looked and the tenderness in his expression on the night of the gala, the night they'd kissed. He looked similar now.

"You have?" she asked. "Even after how we left things?"

Quirking one eyebrow up, he smiled wryly. "I tried to stop thinkin' of you, to forget how perfect you felt in my arms, kissin' me, holdin' me...to force myself to treat you as a friend, nothin' more, since I knew that was what you wanted." He drew in a shuddering breath, holding her gaze with his own. "But Lana, I never could stop dreamin' of you."

Before she could consider her actions — without any real thought at all, other than to get closer — Lana leaned forward and pressed her lips against Mac's. He seemed so surprised that he didn't react for an instant, and she nearly pulled away, but with a growl, he tightened his arms around her, pulling her more firmly against him and deepened the kiss into something utterly sensual...uninhibited. His familiar taste, masculine and almost peppery, exploded in her mouth as he teased her lips with his, stroking his tongue against hers.

"I missed you," she gasped. "I missed this...so much," she finished breathlessly, tangling her fingers in his soft, short hair as she reveled in how amazing his body felt against hers. Mac rubbed his hands under her thin tank top, up and down her bare back, kneading and massaging so that she arched against him with little mewls of pleasure.

She ran her hands along the planes of his chest, then up and along his shoulders, appreciating every dip and exulting in the contented sounds her touch elicited from him. Before she realized what she was doing, she had thrown one leg over his hip so that she straddled his thigh, and she bucked against him, shaking with the intensity of her desire when he pressed deeper into the V of her thighs, right where the center of her pleasure was.

"Oh...oh, Mac," she breathed, clutching at his shoulders so that she flexed her fingers into his muscles.

"You like that, hm?" he asked, his grin just a wicked slash of white before he pressed his thigh to her again.

She gave a wordless cry and arched her back, thrusting her breasts toward him in silent supplication.

"Mm-m, that's what I thought," he answered himself, sounding satisfied with her response, and began to kiss a trail down her neck, even as he stroked his hands from her back to her front to cup the generous mounds of her breasts.

"Ah...ah...oh God, Mac!" She didn't recognize the high-pitched sounds she was making as he strummed his fingers over her tight nipples, pushing herself against him rhythmically, dragging over and over the growing hardness she could feel against her stomach until she thought she might go mad from sensation.

When he snaked one hand down between them, under her thin shorts, to brush her soft mound, which had gone damp and liquid with arousal, her body tightened, passion rising almost impossibly fast. He'd barely begun to touch the bundle of nerves, just circling it with one gentle fingertip, before she felt herself careening over the edge of ecstasy into the most intense orgasm she'd ever had.

"Mac...oh, Mac." She cried out for him blindly, seeking an anchor, and he held onto her tightly.

"It's okay, sugar... I have you... I'm right here," he murmured, drawing out her pleasure so that she was a shuddering, quivering mass in his arms. She thought he might have whispered, "Never gonna let you go," but she couldn't be certain.

When she finally started to come back to herself, he was stroking her sweaty hair away from her forehead.

"I think we should get some rest, now," he said, and she made a sound of protest.

"But I haven't touched you... Don't you, um, want—?"

He interrupted her protest with a sexy chuckle. "Oh, yeah, honey, I definitely want...but not tonight. Seeing your pleasure was enough. My God, Lana, you're glorious, but I can tell you're all worn out." He traced two fingers down her shoulder. "You can barely lift your arm."

She wanted to contradict him, but...he was right. She felt utterly boneless, and exhausted, as if now that he'd given her such an incredible release, all the tension from the past few days had drained away, and she could sleep for a week.

"That was amazing, Mac...like nothing—" She stopped herself awkwardly but decided to continue with her admission anyway. "Like nothing I've ever felt," she whispered.

Mac groaned, his arms tightening around her. "God, Lana...I love hearin' that. Love *knowin'* that."

"Will you stay all night?" she asked.

His body went oddly tense. If she'd been any farther away, he might have fully shuttered his expression, but this close, she could tell he felt uncomfortable.

"What is it?" she prompted.

He shook his head slowly. "How do you always manage to read me?"

She waited silently, wanting to be patient for whatever he was going to say and trying not to worry too much. Frankly, she felt too good to have yet returned to her normal level of tension.

Finally, he answered. "Of course I'll stay, but...ah..." He looked away, and she thought she saw the stain of a dark blush on his cheekbones. "I can't, uh, sleep with my prosthesis on. I've never...never slept next to someone... Well, I mean, not since... You know."

She understood his stumbling speech, and her heart swelled in her chest at the trust he was showing her. "I don't mind at all...totally fine with me," she hurried to assure him, and honestly, she truly found she didn't care, other than the fact that it still caused Mac pain. Otherwise, it was just a part of him. She had come to like all his parts...more than she wanted to admit.

Mac silently turned and slowly removed his prosthesis, with hands that didn't waver for an instant, and his quiet bravery humbled her as much as his trust had. When he stretched back down next to her, she curled around him, snuggling her head into his chest and inhaling his distinctive scent that she couldn't get enough of.

"Good night, darlin'," he murmured.

Sleep was tugging at her so hard that she barely managed to slur, "G'night, Mac," before the world— more peaceful and welcoming than it had been only hours earlier—went dark.

Chapter Eleven

Mac was startled out of a beautiful dream — one involving him and Lana on a desert island, him chasing her along the powder-white sands until he caught her, rolling her underneath him, then...a cold, wet starfish prodded his face, touching his cheek, then his lip. He came to wakefulness as suddenly as he usually did, but it took him a moment to process what he was seeing. There was a little freckled face with a bright stare, right in front of his eyes, covered with a mop of unruly orange curls...but who the hell was short enough? And why did it look like it was scarcely past dawn? Memories of Gray and the day before filtered back in, as the little boy leaned forward and prodded him again with a hand that felt suspiciously damp.

"I peed my bed," Gray confided in a sort of stage whisper, which he probably thought was quiet but which was anything but.

Horror curled in Mac's stomach. Did he now have little-boy piss in two places on his face? There was definitely some dampness on his lip.

Gray had more to say, though. "I went to the bathroom and got my cup and a towel, to clean it up…and now my whole bed is a puddle, and I can't sleep."

Lana's soft form—and damn, her curves felt too good for him to be noticing them in front of a three-year-old kid—shifted on the bed behind him, and he felt the pressure of her hand as she pushed up to look over his shoulder.

"Gray, baby, what did we say about leaving your room when it's still nighttime?" she asked, her voice still husky with sleep.

The little boy pushed his lower lip out. "But it's all *wet*," he complained. His chin had a suspicious-looking quiver. Mac heaved an inward sigh. He was definitely not getting back to acting out any part of that dream with Lana any time soon.

"Why don't I come take a look, okay?" he offered, clearing the lingering sleepy scratchiness from his throat as he spoke.

"Okay, Mac," Gray agreed readily, and the completely trusting way the little boy spoke tugged at something inside of Mac, making him want to do everything in his power to live up to the grateful way Gray was looking at him.

When he darted a glance back at Lana, stretched out on the bed like some sort of Greek goddess but with a shining look of gratitude beaming from her face, the sensation merely intensified. He only hoped he was worthy.

"Oooh, you got a picture on your chest!" Gray exclaimed excitedly, putting his moist hand on Mac's tattoo.

"Oh, wow," Lana echoed. "That's, ah, really large. I guess with the low light, I didn't notice...although I can't believe I could have missed it."

Her attempt at tactfulness was nothing short of adorable.

Mac puffed up his chest and shot her a grin. "Well, now, you might have been a bit distracted, too," he said in a conciliatory tone, and he narrowly missed the small throw pillow that she lobbed at him.

"It's from my Navy days, as you might guess. Early on in them, in fact, when I thought I was invincible, and I was all but brimmin' with patriotism." He lightly touched the enormous eagle and American flag, underlined by a curling red ribbon reading 'Semper Fortis', which were blazoned over his heart for all eternity. "I'm still just as proud — don't get me wrong — but I'm no longer as susceptible to drinking a bottle of tequila with my shipmates and heading to the tattoo parlor together," he finished, his grin growing wry.

"You must love eagles," Gray observed, and Mac couldn't contain his bark of laughter.

"Well, as a matter of fact, I do find them to be quite a noble bird," he answered, and Lana's eyes shone with hidden amusement.

"Lana has a picture on her body, too," Gray piped up, and Lana gave a strangled sort of squawk.

"Does she now?" Mac drawled, raking his eyes along her form. "I can't say that I've ever noticed, so I think it must be someplace I haven't seen."

"Keep talking like that, Lieutenant Commander MacKenzie, and you never will," she returned with a snap in her voice, and he felt his body zing with awareness.

Oh yeah, I love it when my Lana gets prickly. The thought drew him up short, though. *My Lana.* He liked the sound of that way too much…and he had to admit, if only to himself, that if he'd only been *falling* for her before, after last night, he might now have fully *fallen*. Unfortunately, he had skimpy evidence to show whether she felt the same way. What he did know, though—and why she'd called him here—was that she and Gray still needed his help and protection. After what they'd discovered the night before, that was glaringly obvious. They might even need him now more than ever.

He sat up, a bit more awkwardly than usual, given his audience of two, trying not feel self-conscious about the stump of his leg being exposed by his shorts, however briefly. Gray watched the process of him pulling on his liner, sock, sleeve and finally his prosthetic leg itself with avid interest. Lana, for her part, was silent. He figured she was probably trying to give him space.

His heart sank when the little boy opened his mouth, and he braced himself. There was nobody who could match a young child for brutal honesty. His oldest nephew had shied away from him at first.

"You got a robot leg! That's so cool!" Gray exclaimed, and his little face practically glowed with admiration.

The relief that Mac felt—swiftly followed by amusement—was staggering. He could have handled any response, but man, this one was an unexpected joy. He dared a glance back at Lana, and her lovely face radiated quiet happiness, her eyes suspiciously misty.

He gave her hand a swift squeeze before he followed Gray to see what he could do to clean up the sodden bed.

As the pair went to Gray's room together, Lana could hear the preschooler peppering Mac with questions. Did they make his robo-leg just for him? Was he now a cyborg? Did he like superheroes? Transformers?

Laughing to herself, she forced her tired body to move so she could get up and dressed to help Mac. Even though she'd slept better last night than she had for quite a while, it still wasn't enough to totally make up the balance of her sleep deficit, and she was dragging. When she checked her phone and saw that it was only just past six in the morning, she felt better. Good Lord, a month earlier, when she'd just been worried about her society and philanthropic work, getting up at six would have been unthinkable.

Deciding from the continuous happy chatter that Mac sounded like he'd be okay for a little longer alone with Gray, she zipped into her connected bathroom and got ready quickly, brushing her teeth and hair and washing her face. If she took the time to spritz on just a hint of her favorite perfume and to dab on some mascara and lip gloss, that was nobody's business but her own. Still, as she pulled on a pair of well-worn jeans and a soft cashmere sweater, she grew pensive.

Last night was a mistake...wasn't it? Was it? She wished she felt as certain as she had been before. Her feelings that Mac was an amazing man—good and kind, deserving of the best—hadn't changed. If anything, the more time she spent with him, and the more she saw his courage, the more strongly she felt for him. If he deserved the best, she *knew* it wasn't her. *What if he wants you anyway?* that small, secret hopeful voice, the one she'd thought had been killed when she was a young teenager, whispered. It was a tantalizing idea.

She mentally replayed their interactions from the day and night before. Oh God, when he'd rushed into the room like some sort of righteous knight, hellbent on protecting her, she didn't know if she'd ever seen anyone so wonderful. But then, when he'd held her gently, touching her with patience and sensual knowledge, he'd been nothing short of irresistible. Her face heated at the memory of how responsive she'd been, how quick to climax. And she'd never felt anything like that...either the pleasure or how cherished he'd made her feel. Now that she'd had the feeling once, she was no longer certain she could bear to give him up a second time — not when doing so would obviously cause them both so much pain.

Still, if she didn't give him up — and God, she really wasn't sure if she could — then she would have to confess the truth to him, and that might be scariest thing of all. She would have to reveal the very worst of herself, lay it out there in the open for him to take or leave, and she would be giving him the power to destroy her. And yet...without meaning to, hadn't she already started to do that very thing? Caring for him as she did, would she really ever have been able to walk away unscathed?

She blew out a hard breath, twisting her hair into a tighter braid than she'd needed to. As she looked in the mirror, she knew the truth. Something had changed between them, and she wasn't sorry, even if she should be. If he gave her one hint — *just one* — that he might still be willing, she was going to try to find the courage to fight for him.

When she popped her head into Gray's room, the bed looked freshly made with plaid sheets and a quilt, and Mac was wrangling the little boy into yet another yacht-club-appropriate outfit, complete with sweater. She had to admit that she was impressed, and she thought that there was certainly something to be said for military discipline.

"You work fast," she said, her tone genuinely admiring. She'd always been someone who thought she'd had real sympathy for mothers and other caregivers when she saw them on flights, out shopping or even at the occasional restaurant or café, but becoming Gray's guardian had taught her that she had barely understood anything about how hard being a full-time caregiver to anyone could be. It was especially true of someone so young that they couldn't always express themselves without dissolving into tears and rage.

"Years of experience in the service, ma'am," Mac returned jauntily, then cocked his head to one side. "Well, and I will admit to a small bit of bribery."

"Mac promised if I was a good listener, I can touch his robot leg," Gray interjected, speaking as soon as his head popped out of the collar of the sweater Mac had been wrestling him into.

Lana giggled. She loved seeing this side of Mac…and the open admiration on Gray's face, too.

"All's fair in love and preschooler-wrangling," she quipped. "We grown-ups have to seize any slight advantage we have."

"I'm going to remember that you said that, Ms. Fitzhugh," Mac answered, the look in his apple-green eyes growing warm, and she knew he was focusing on the first part of the saying she'd adapted.

She clucked purposefully, motioning toward Gray. "Now that you're ready, Gray, do you want to come help me cook breakfast while Mac gets dressed, too?"

Gray looked like he might want to argue, so she sweetened the pot. "I'll let you choose whatever breakfast you want."

That got his attention, as she'd known it would. She'd recently discovered that, for whatever reason, Sam and Cain had apparently strongly favored smoothies for breakfast, so the world of pancakes and waffles was entirely new to the little boy, and he was absolutely enamored.

"French toast?" he asked, his voice nearly reverent when he said the words. Lana hid her smile.

"Sure," she agreed readily, and Gray nearly ran toward her, falling over himself with helpfulness. Unfortunately, he was what she mentally called 'aggressively helpful' in the kitchen, so most of cooking with him involved her preventing him from burning his fingers off, but he seemed to enjoy it, and it certainly provided a distraction from other, sadder thoughts.

By the time Mac came down, they had prepared a copious amount of the ugliest French toast she'd ever seen. Lana was simply grateful that neither she nor Gray had gotten hurt. Mac—bless him—exclaimed over the breakfast like it was the most delicious, food-magazine-worthy dish he'd ever eaten, and Gray just soaked up the praise like soil in a drought.

When Gray went to play with his blocks again in the other room, still in Lana's sight, she and Mac shared cleaning up the kitchen in a companionable silence. As she was finishing the final wipe-down of the table, she felt more than saw Mac come up next to her.

"Thanks again for a wonderful breakfast," he rumbled.

"Gray can't hear you now, so you don't have to pretend," she returned light-heartedly.

Mac shook his head. "Wasn't pretendin'. I mean, I'll admit it wasn't the prettiest, but it sure tasted delicious…and you're wonderful with Gray, so patient as you teach him."

Feeling her cheeks flush with pleasure at the compliment, Lana hastened to change the subject. "Any word from your friend, the Viking-looking security guy?"

Mac chuckle was rich and low, rolling into the room. "Oh, man, can I tell him you called him that? Gun would love it… He's apparently a big fan of yours, you know? Well, your family, anyway. And it's all quiet with the systems, although he's gonna come pick up the device we found last night to see if he can glean anything more from it. He's got a buddy lookin' into your friends' accident, too."

Lana had been feeling a warm amusement at Mac's description, but with his last words, it felt as if ice water had been injected directly into her veins. She groped for the chair back of on the of the dining room chairs and sank down onto it, her knees suddenly weak. "Oh my God…you think it wasn't an accident?" Her voice was more of a croak.

"I didn't say that," Mac answered, sounding cautious. "Just…if someone is really going after you and Gray, it has to be about either you or Gray, so we gotta look at all the angles. Such a shocking family tragedy... It's certainly worth at least looking into, don't you think?"

"But surely the police—" she started.

"—did a thorough investigation. I'm in no way implying that they didn't, but they don't have the additional information that we know now." Mac's voice was calm, and his large, warm hand on her shoulder was reassuring.

"I just... It would be so *horrible*, Mac," she said, knowing she wasn't being articulate, but he seemed to understand anyway.

"Yeah, sugar, it would...but it wouldn't be your fault or Gray's. It would solely be the fault of whoever is behind this, whatever all *this* turns out to be."

They stayed like that for a moment, her sitting and his standing behind her, lending her his strength.

"I really wish, now more than anything, that I'd found the courage to apologize to Sam. I know I mentioned we argued and became estranged. We had a big falling-out, in fact, years ago. I always meant to—thought I would have time to—but then she was just gone." Her throat felt thick with tears. "It was awful enough, thinking that they had an accident, but now..." She trailed off, unable to finish the thought.

"Darlin', I can't pretend to know what passed between you, although I'm willin' to listen anytime you want to talk about it, but I do know that I saw that sweet picture of the two of you in her office," he answered.

"Yeah...when I first arrived and asked Gray if he knew who I was, he walked right over to the picture, pointed me out and called me Auntie Lala," she recalled, smiling mistily again at the memory.

"Did you happen to notice what the date was on the will, when it was read?"

Lana half-turned her head to look at him questioningly. "Ah…actually, yes, it was almost four years ago. I remember because I had the thought that they must have drawn up a new will right after they had Gray."

"And how long ago was your falling-out with Sam?" he prompted.

Lana felt silly that she hadn't done the math herself. Although Lana had mentally linked the guardianship to her childhood promise, obviously Sam had written it on a legal document much more recently.

"I see where you're going with this, and you're right. You're absolutely right. She and I argued twelve years ago, after I did something unforgivable."

"Well, now, I don't believe she thought it was unforgivable," he answered, and her eyes filled with hot tears that spilled over onto her cheeks.

She'd suspected that Sam might have started to forgive her, but of course, Sam must have truly forgiven her nearly four years earlier, looking at her baby boy and naming Lana, of all people, his guardian if something happened to both Sam and Cain. Had Sam wanted to mend things as badly as Lana had? Lana would likely never know for sure, but Mac's logic had given her the confidence to believe.

"If it wasn't an accident…" Lana's breath hitched before she steadied herself enough to continue. "If it wasn't, then I want justice…for all the time that Gray will miss out on, but also all the time I will," she finished.

Mac settled down onto the chair next to her, brushing away the tears on her cheeks with his thumbs in a curiously intimate gesture. "If we find anything pointing in that direction, Lana, you'll have my help every step of the way," he replied, and it sounded like a vow.

The room was so quiet that Lana could hear the ticking of the antique grandfather clock in the living room, and Gray's little squeaks and 'vrooms' as he moved the blocks around with total absorption in his play.

"Did you have anything on the schedule for today?" Mac finally broke the silence by asking.

Lana knew that the eyes she turned on him must be worried. "Do you think it's safe? For us still to go out, now that we know…that it wasn't me?"

Mac blew out a breath, and his expression turned stony. "The way I see it, we can stay here, inside, waiting, but also risking being surprised where we think we're safe…or we can carry on as usual, knowing to be watchful because you and Gray will be much more of a target if we're away from the house."

It made sense, and Lana thought she understood where he was going with it. "If we stay locked up in the house, the person might stop so we never know who he was, or we might be betrayed when we don't expect it, but if we go out, we might draw him or her out, is that it?"

"I actually don't like the sound of it, now that you're repeatin' it to me. Can I take everythin' back so we stay here, safe, and call the police and probably also your family?" Mac's tone was light, but she could tell that if she decided that they should lock themselves up in the house like a fortress, he'd be totally onboard.

Lana was thoughtful, truly wanting to give the right consideration to everything. "Just like we talked about before, we can't call the police until we have some sort of evidence. They won't believe us."

"They might if you or your family threw your weight around," Mac suggested, raising his eyebrows.

Lana pursed her lips. "Sure, they'd outwardly cooperate — if I were willing to involve my family, which is a huge *if* — but I still don't think they'd truly believe us without more proof." She drummed her fingers on the table, her light-pink nails making a quiet '*dit-dit-dit-dit-dit*' sound on the wooden table's surface. "Nope...I like your idea."

"Don't call it *my* idea... I'm disowning it as an idea. It's an orphan idea now, one that might turn out terribly if anything at all goes wrong."

She read true concern on his face, but it also made the most sense to proceed this way.

"We'll have to make sure that nothing goes wrong, then, hm?" she prompted. "Maybe we can call your friends again?"

Lips twitching, even though it was clear he was trying to look stern, Mac only managed an expression of mild exasperation...mingled with a sort of reluctant pride. "I do believe I've been a bad influence on you, sugar."

She gave him a saucy grin in return.

"I'll call my friends...or I guess I should confess now that they've never really been that far away. Lana, I know that you're dead-set against involving your brothers or your grandfather, and I totally understand not wanting to upset Pat, but do you really think it would make your brothers lose respect for you, havin' you ask for help?"

The question was a good one, and Lana forced herself to step back from the issue, to think it about it logically instead of emotionally. Mac was right that Fitz might very well understand — and be royally pissed off at Mac for not calling him sooner—but this could also be the straw that broke the very fragile understanding they'd reached. Plus, her middle brother might be truly out of range and was enjoying some well-deserved bonding time with his young family. She supposed there were always ways to get in touch, but no...she held firm.

Her relationship with Drew was even more complicated. While Fitz had escaped the pressures of their family legacy and the ugly underbelly of the truth of how their parents had treated them by joining the Marine Corps, Drew had stuck things out. He'd almost gone about it in a completely opposite way, but with the same sort of result. The happy, witty, mischievous boy she'd once adored had grown into a rigidly proper man, suspicious of everyone and everything and determined to keep everyone in line, especially his family. Or rather, his wayward sister...since Lord knew, nobody could control Pat. She understood why Drew had been deeply disappointed in her behavior as a teen, and he had only granted her the most grudging respect as an adult, in spite of all the good she'd tried to do in the world. He took his position as CEO and Chairman of the Board of Directors of Fitzhugh Manufacturing incredibly seriously, at the expense of almost anything else, including fun or humor, she often thought.

"I...ah, no...we still need to do this without them," she answered firmly, intending to put an end to the line of thought.

She should have known that Mac would see more than she expected, though. "I'm gonna listen to you, even though Fitz is likely to roast my balls over an open firepit if I let anything happen to his baby sister...but

Lana, was what you did really so bad that you truly think your brothers still struggle to forgive you?" He put his hand over one of hers on the table, stilling her fingers. "I mean, I have two sisters, and there's hardly anything I wouldn't forgive them for. I'd walk through fire for them, and believe me, I am well aware that they aren't perfect."

A flood of emotions washed over her, including the familiar old shame, regret, sadness, determination to be better...but at the center was her anger and disappointment in her own mother and father. "It's...complicated," she admitted. "Let's go enjoy this gorgeous day, just one more, then I promise I'll confess the worst of myself to you tonight."

She felt as if she were bargaining with the universe as well as with Mac. Could she have just one more day, one more memory, before laying herself bare? Before she changed everything, and maybe Mac no longer looked at her with the warmth and tenderness she'd grown accustomed to? That she craved more than anything?

"One more day, darlin'. Of course," he answered.

"All right then," she replied, satisfied, and checked the forecast on her phone. With the strength of the sunlight streaming in the skylights, it was going to be a rare true spring day in Minnesota. There was usually only about a week of spring every year, shoehorned between winter and summer.

"Looks like it's going to be really nice today! I'll just run up and change into a skirt," she said enthusiastically.

"Um, I don't know if we saw the same weather report, but it's only gonna be about sixty-four degrees out," Mac answered cautiously.

Lana nodded, practically jumping off her seat. "Yeah, exactly. Sixty-four and sunny is glorious for this time of year!" she enthused.

Mac's smile was bemused. "Must be a Minnesota thing...but sure, we can wait. I'm never gonna turn down a chance to admire your legs, honey." As she ran upstairs, she could hear him talking with another friend about security.

Chapter Twelve

The weather sure was different from Georgia, where it was already so steamy that it felt like summer, but Mac had to admit that the freshness of the Minnesota spring was incredibly pleasant. The air was cool, smelling clean and somehow new, and flowers were just starting to bloom everywhere they looked. Even better, though, Lana and Gray were both in high spirits as they set off on the path that would take them around one of the Minneapolis lakes the city was so famous for, and their enthusiasm was contagious.

"Did you remember the goose food?" Gray asked, for at least the tenth time. The repetition did nothing to dim Mac's mood, though.

"Sure did, buddy. It's in my backpack, along with our picnic. Lots of yummy oats, grapes and vegetable peels for some lucky geese," Mac answered easily. "Although I wouldn't have known that bread wasn't allowed anymore if you two hadn't told me," he confessed.

The warmth of Lana's smile, even though he couldn't see her eyes behind her large paparazzi-deterrent sunglasses, was worth all the extra time he'd taken to cut up their grapes into quarters...for the damn geese. Although in all fairness, he knew he'd have had to cut them up anyway to be safe for Gray, too.

"I suppose there's always more to learn about safety," he observed. "My older sister nearly tackled me to the ground when I tried to put her eldest into the car without a booster seat, and the kid is over four feet tall—which is apparently not tall enough." He snorted at the memory. "When I was a kid, I swear my daddy just put me in the back of the convertible with a bungee cord," he added, and Lana's laugh was silvery as it floated back to him on the breeze.

"I'm glad he didn't go over any big bumps, then. There are definitely a lot more safety rules now," Lana agreed. "I had to do a sort of crash course, myself, although of course I've been learning a lot by spending a ton of time with my darling niece."

"How is baby Hope, then?" Mac asked, catching up to her so they could walk together on the path. Gray had been holding her hand, but now that the walkway had widened, she'd let the little boy go ahead at his own meandering pace, stopping frequently to admire a particular flower or piece of grass.

"She's adorable—just like her mom, of course—and Fitz couldn't be prouder." Judging from the pride in her voice, her brother wasn't the only member of the Fitzhugh family who was impressed by baby Hope.

"I've never seen Fitz so happy...or two people so perfect for each other," Mac remarked, and Lana made a noise of agreement.

"I know that you and Fitz met at the hospital, but I don't know much more than that," Lana said in a casual tone, but Mac could tell it was a leading question.

"Hm, you sure you really want to hear this?" Mac asked. "It doesn't always make the two of us look so good."

They paused as Lana admired a tiny little white flower that Gray had brought her before he ran off again.

"Well, now I *definitely* want to know," she quipped, and her smile was irreverent.

"All right...well, I had been at the rehab hospital about six months —"

Lana gasped. "Six months?" She looked horrified. "What? I mean, that's so long!"

"It is...believe me, it *felt* long. Considerin' we were ambushed, though, I'm lucky to be alive at all, especially since I had a head injury as well." Mac normally disliked talking about his past in any detail, especially the attack that had cost him his foot and part of his leg, but with Lana, he found he didn't mind so much. More, he *wanted* her to know this part of him.

"When I first got there, I had a bad attitude — not too uncommon, in fact — but by the time your brother arrived, I was sort of like the grandfather of the group. I understood his anger, frustration...pain, all of it. The feeling like you failed, somehow, by survivin' when so many others didn't make it back, although he likely had it harder than me with the greater losses to his unit and the extensive burns and reconstructive surgeries."

Lana was silent for a long moment, and when he looked over, she was hanging her head. When he pushed her sunglasses back onto the top of her head, her eyes were red from the tears streaking down her face. His chest felt suddenly too small to hold his heart, and he fought the urge to pull her into his arms.

"Aw, now, darlin'...why are you cryin'? You know this story has a happy endin'."

She sniffled, looking miserable...and horribly guilty. "Fitz—Colin—never told us. We knew he was in the hospital for a while, but he didn't...didn't want us to know. I had no idea how much pain he'd been in."

"Look... I know there's some history between Fitz and your family, but I also know that lots of guys go out of their way to spare their family knowin' details, and I can say with certainty that he wouldn't want you to feel guilty. I downplayed everything to my sisters, too—not that they ever listened to me—but I know I'd never hurt them for the world."

She gave a watery sniff and they started walking again, going faster to catch up to Gray, although with how slow he walked, he'd barely gotten ahead of them.

"I want to hear the rest," Lana said, and Mac only hesitated for a moment before continuing.

"As I said, when I first got there, I was all messed up...not just my body, but my mind...and I guess, my soul, too—or whatever you want to call it. I was bitter over everythin' I thought I'd lost, every day was painful and it was hard to fight through. I was lashin' out at everyone around me, even my sisters when they visited." It was a dark time to return to, even in his mind, but it wasn't as painful as it had once been.

"What changed?" she asked, as they stopped to let Gray explore a clearing where a bunch of stumps and rocks were laid out in patterns.

Mac's laugh was humorless. "Oddly enough, a letter from my ex-fiancée."

"Uh, *what*? You were *engaged*?" Lana asked, her expression growing stormy. "Did that woman leave you because of what happened to you?" she demanded angrily, and the righteous indignation on his behalf was enough to warm him all over.

"Yes, I was engaged once…but no, she did not leave me because I got hurt. We ended things — I *forced* her to end things — a long time ago." Now he felt the familiar twinge of regret and shame at the man he'd once been. "She was my high school sweetheart, and she was gentle and loyal, but I thought I was too good for her…too good to keep my promises to her, so I treated her like dirt." He couldn't look at Lana as he spoke, wanting to get it all out.

"I stopped respondin' to her letters and calls, and when she visited that last time, I all but called her names in front of the other guys. I'm not proud of the man I was then." He could still see Hannah's face, tear-streaked, as she'd told him she couldn't marry him, couldn't be with him any longer, and he remembered the satisfaction he'd felt at the time that he'd been relieved of such a burden.

"I told you she was loyal, though, and real kind. I was feelin' sorry for myself, bein' alone in the hospital — no wife, no fiancée, no girlfriend for longer than about three dates, either — and I got a letter from Hannah and her kids. She wrote that she and her new husband had run into Kim in town and heard about my bein' injured, that they were thinkin' of and prayin' for me and that the kids had wanted to make me some medals, to hang up in my hospital room, since they knew I was so brave. In that moment, readin' about the generosity of spirit of a woman who I was so bad to, and her sweet little babies who wanted to make me fancy pictures, dripping with those stick-on sequins and jewels that you can find in craft stores, I was humbled." He paused, taking a breath.

"Not in a bad way, though," he hurried to explain. "I understood that I was lucky. It still sucked — oh hell, did it suck — but I suddenly felt more hopeful somehow, like this was my chance to change and do whatever I wanted for the rest of my life. And I started sorta taking the other new guys who came to hospital under my wing."

"Like my brother," Lana guessed quietly.

Mac nodded. "Exactly like your brother. I had learned that rehab after a horrible injury is pretty damn awful, but that you can get through it, one day at a time, one hour at a time. Fitz and I became friends, maybe because we had so much in common, and he told me I made things a little easier for him. I would make appointments to meet up with him for dinner, to play cards, to work out. It's a lot harder to skip an appointment with a buddy than with a doctor or therapist. When I was released, he put me in touch with your grandfather, which was great for me since not everyone wants to hire a pilot with only one regular leg, and well, you know the rest of the story."

"Thank you for telling me," Lana said, slipping her hand into his, where it felt exactly right. "For trusting me," she added.

"Well, you asked…and I did say I wanted to tell you the truth," he answered simply.

They walked down the path in silence for a while, but it was a comfortable silence, filled with the sound of the lake rippling in the breeze, the wind through the surrounding trees, the birds chirping and warbling. It was funny, but he could actually hear the difference between the birds here and those in Georgia...and he realized he hadn't really spent much time listening before.

"Is that why you made your vow...that if you ever started to feel something for someone again, you would let her know...and be there for her?" she asked suddenly, and Mac was impressed again at how intuitive she was.

"Yeah, that's part of it. But even if I hadn't made that vow, I'm not sure there's any world in which I wouldn't have wanted to be there for you, Lana." He made the confession in a low voice, but he could tell by the way she stiffened that she'd heard him.

"You shouldn't say that until you've heard everything," she cautioned. He wished he could punch the crap out of whoever had hurt her so badly, made her feel so worthless.

"Okay then, I'll wait...but I'm warnin' you. I don't think it's gonna change my mind."

She said something so quietly he couldn't be certain he'd heard correctly, but he thought she'd said, "That's what I'm hoping."

He didn't have a chance to ask, then, as Gray ran back to them, excitedly pointing at the rowboats leaving from a small rental place.

"Look at the ships! Can we go on a ship? Please, please, please!" Gray was so animated that he was nearly bouncing with it.

When Lana turned a questioning look at him, he shrugged helplessly. "What kind of a Navy man would I be if I didn't take the boy out on a boat on a day like today?"

"Yay!" Gray cheered, only pausing to turn back for a second. "I'm the captain," he announced, and Mac and Lana both burst out laughing.

* * * *

It was what Lana liked to think of as a Golden Day — one of those glorious, perfect days that she thought might live in her memory forever with the sound of Gray's laughter, the feel of Mac's hand in hers, the mingled scents of the lake, budding trees and spring itself. They rowed around the lake for an hour. Well, really, Mac rowed while she and Gray crewed, *poorly*, but Mac didn't seem to mind. Lana just congratulated herself on keeping Gray from falling in, since the little boy had been so excited that he'd kept standing up, waving his arms and generally rocking the boat as much as possible.

She'd feared they might all have a touch of seasickness — *lakesickness? Was that a thing? A word?* — afterward, so instead of finding a spot to picnic, they'd opted to feed the geese next. And by geese, she really meant evil avian hell-spawn. Watching one of the surprisingly large birds hiss at, then chase Gray, when they'd been too slow getting the bag of goose food out of the backpack had been quite a different experience from the placid, bucolic scene she'd pictured. Still, after they'd flung most of the food in one go at the geese, who had been circling them before they'd escaped to higher ground, Gray had pronounced feeding the geese as, 'very fun', so she was counting that as a win, too.

Finally, they'd found a beautiful picnic table, set back a good distance from the lake and path, well into the trees, but on higher ground so they could still look out onto the water. They'd set up the full spread of the food she'd packed, including sandwiches, potato salad, macaroni salad, Caesar salad, Jell-O salad and of course, fruit salad.

"So…is everything on this table considered a salad?" Mac asked, his eyes dancing with amusement.

"Hm…well, yeah, I guess so…except for the sandwiches," she answered.

"What kind are they?" he asked, and she narrowed her eyes suspiciously at his leading tone.

"Chicken salad," she answered.

He snorted. "I rest my case."

She managed to hold in her laughter, but she couldn't hide her smile. "Well-played," she admitted, fixing plates for the three of them.

"Mm-m…so delicious, as usual," Mac moaned after taking his first few bites. "I'll admit I was skeptical about the Jell-O salad, because anythin' that calls itself salad but also contains Cool Whip and marshmallows seems kinda wrong to me, on a molecular level, but that's absolutely delectable."

She chuckled, spearing a grapefruit chunk covered in coconut with her fork. "Serves you right for making fun of salad while in the state of Minnesota. In fact, I'd bet there's not much that *couldn't* become salad if you make it properly."

Lana had always thought that preschoolers were supposed to be picky eaters, but while Gray ate much smaller portions than an adult, he generally seemed to like most things she served him. Now, when she looked over at him, he was wolfing down his entire plate as if he thought she would snatch it away from him at any moment.

"You...are really not what I expected," Mac admitted. "I mean, I know that when we first met, we were planning a fancy party, and so a lot of our conversation was around the gala, and your family, but..." He trailed off.

"But what?" she prompted.

"I really had you pegged for more of a caviar and bacon-wrapped scallops kind of lady," he answered at last, seeming almost sheepish.

"Oh, that." She waved her hands as if to wave the words away. "I mean, I guess I am...or I always was. It's how I grew up, with fancy hors d'oeuvres like foie gras and caviar at every event, ice sculptures, sushi — which by the way, is a much bigger deal to get fresh here, away from the coast — petits-fours and macarons. I didn't even know that people served water that wasn't carbonated until I was probably nine or ten. When I was really little, my mother would dress me up and take me with her to all sorts of events, almost like an accessory. I was...grateful to spend the time with her."

She didn't know why she'd mentioned her mother, but she hurried to switch back to talking about the safer subject of parties. "As I got older, the parties I decided to attend changed a bit — lots more fundraisers than just extravagant events — but I still have a walk-in closet just for my ballgowns and another one for my shoes."

Mac made a strangled sound that could have been shock, and she raised one eyebrow, daring him to comment.

"However, since I graduated from college, I've also done a lot more hands-on work, which has included a fair number of potluck dinners at churches, shelters and community centers. It's actually the reason I started learning how to cook, so I could have dishes to bring without bothering our chef. Of course, Marcel still insisted on teaching me—he's our long-time French-Canadian chef, hired by my grandfather since my grandmother could barely boil water." She smiled at the memory. "And now, of course, Marcel really only cooks for my grandfather, and we have a sous-chef to cook for Drew…when he's around, that is. I've been cooking for myself for years, making the occasional dish for big dinners or just for the staff, which is lucky since it means I can cook for Gray and me now."

Mac looked at her for such a long time that she started to fidget. They were so far back from the path that she'd taken her hat and glasses off as they ate, allowing Gray to do the same, figuring that they were safe from photographers at the moment. Unfortunately, that left her with no protection from Mac's stare, which felt like it might see too much—certainly more than she'd intended.

"What? Do I have Jell-O on my nose?" she ventured, and Mac shook his head slowly.

"No, your nose is just as adorable as it always is, but…you continue to surprise me, darlin'."

Uncomfortable with his scrutiny—and she certainly didn't know why she should be, since people had been staring at her for as long as she could remember and often judging her harshly—she stood up too quickly to serve more lemonade. Three things happened simultaneously. First, she tumbled backward over the bench of the picnic table and onto the grassy clearing behind. Second, Mac ran to help her, carefully kneeling on the ground and cradling her in his arms. She was mortified to notice that, as she fell, her skirt had hiked up until it barely covered her underwear, leaving most of her thighs exposed, and her hair had come undone and hung haphazardly around her shoulders. Finally, just when Mac would have helped her up, she heard a sound that she'd learned to loathe and resent, even as she'd tried to make the best of her unasked-for position as a member of the Fitzhugh family. It was the unmistakable click of the shutter of a long-range camera, one of the really expensive ones. As she looked up, sure enough, there was someone—a young man this time—standing in the bushes leading from the path to the clearing where they'd eaten.

She struggled to her feet as quickly as possible, and Mac's touches were nothing other than completely innocent—gentlemanly, even—but she knew how it would look in the click-bait headlines. With new technology, the press didn't even have to wait for the next issue of whatever magazine. They could put things up online instantly.

"What is it, sugar? Are you okay? You seem dazed," Mac said, his voice heavy with worry.

"There was a photographer...just there," she pointed, knowing her words sounded wooden but unable to care.

"Sneaky bastard!" Mac exclaimed. To her horror, she heard Gray echo it from the table behind in a sing-song.

"Sneaky bastard, sneaky bastard, sneaky bastard."

Mac groaned. "I'm sorry, honey. I'll go chase him down for you, though. What did he look like?"

She shrugged, feeling like she carried a thousand pounds on her shoulders. "It doesn't matter. He probably already uploaded everything somewhere. There's really no stopping them. I've mostly just given up, only I *so* wanted today just for us."

Mac tipped her chin up with one strong, tanned finger so that she was forced to meet his eyes, and his expression was fierce. "He will *not* take this away from us, Lana. Nobody can. Today is *ours*...and any other day. *We* choose...not them."

She felt tears sting her eyes and back of her throat, but his passion was contagious. Something about his defiant attitude made her body thrill, and she thought again what a formidable asset he must have been to the Navy.

"We choose," she echoed.

"I'm not embarrassed by anythin' we did today, and you shouldn't be either," Mac continued firmly. "I only hope that interloper had the decency not to get Gray in the picture."

Lana forced herself to push down her own upset and think logically. "He probably doesn't know who Gray is," she said, hoping it wasn't just wishful thinking. "But pictures of Fitzhughs always sell. I try not to blame them—the photographers—but sometimes, like today, when they purposely wait to catch me at my worst, it's really hard not to."

"There are guys from Gun's crew keeping an eye out for us. They can probably still get him. They've only been watchin' for anyone gettin' close." Mac sounded the way she sometimes felt in these situations, which was helpless and frustrated about it.

She understood. "And of course, with a powerful zoom lens, a photographer doesn't physically need to approach us. It's okay. It really isn't worth pursuing, since the pictures are probably already in someone's cloud server or email. It's just bad luck." Maybe if she repeated it to herself and Mac long enough, she would believe it. The most she could hope for now was that her brother Drew wouldn't see the pictures from Germany.

Chapter Thirteen

They were subdued as they packed up the remnants of the picnic, and Lana hated it, but a bit of the shine had gone out of the day, although she refused to let it be spoiled entirely. Still, by mutual consent — and because Gray was yawning with increasing frequency — they headed back home. Lana wasn't sure exactly when she'd started thinking of it that way, but the Erasmus family house felt like home, and she felt a surge of affection as she saw the lines of the familiar mansion come into sight.

Unsurprisingly, Gray had nodded off in the car, and Mac carried him up to his bedroom without so much as breathing heavily, a feat Lana tried — and failed — not to be envious of. She'd just put away the contents of the backpack and was pouring herself and Mac the long-delayed lemonade into tall, cut-crystal glasses when her phone rang.

Without looking, she knew who it would be, and the caller ID confirmed it.

"Hi, Drew," she said brightly. "How are you? How's Munich? Have you gotten to see those friends of Granda's yet?"

"Lana, you know why I'm calling," her brother replied tersely, and suddenly, she felt like she was back in high school, begging again for Drew not to send her away to a boarding school for wayward girls, pleading with him that she could change.

"No, I actually don't know, but I'm guessing you're eager to tell me," she answered flippantly, knowing it would anger him.

"A colleague at this conference showed me a picture of you, one that's apparently currently going viral, because she was worried. Can you deny you were practically on top of that pilot friend of Fitz's today?" Drew's voice was harsh, and Lana's shoulders slumped. She felt the same sense of sinking into quicksand that always seemed to overcome her when she spoke to her oldest brother, but she refused to let him think the worst without an explanation.

"I was with Mac, yes, but I would hardly call it 'all over him.' We were —"

Drew cut her off. "That's not what it looks like in the picture, and there are a couple different angles. That skirt you're wearing is so short it might as well —"

This time, it was her turn to cut him off. "It was *hiked up*! I had just fallen, and Mac was helping me up when some creepy photographer invaded our privacy."

Drew continued as if she hadn't spoken. "Every time I think you've changed, I see some more new suggestive pictures in the press."

"Because they make them look that way to sell better!" Lana protested, growing even more frustrated.

Drew hadn't even paused. "It's the same acting out crap you did when you were a teenager, trying to pick up where mother left off by making headlines any way she could, sleeping around..."

At that, Lana heard a low growl behind her, and realized that Drew had been speaking so loudly that Mac must have also heard every word.

"Put him on speaker phone," Mac ordered, his voice dark...menacing. She didn't even try to argue.

"Hey Drew, it's Mac, that pilot friend of Fitz's." Mac's voice was deceptively calm and silky. "I just wanted to point out that you've interrupted or spoken over your sister—your sister who, just like all your family, you should respect and cherish above all others—three times in a row now. You're angry about a risk to your family's reputation, fine. I can understand that...but you didn't listen to a word she said, which was nothing but the truth, by the way. You went too far by acting like you have the right to judge her choice of who she wants to be intimate with, though, which—now that she's an adult, and has been for a long damn time—is just as much your business as it is a strange photographer's...which is *not. At. All.*"

Drew was silent on the other end of the line, and she wished it were a video call so she could read his expression.

As she watched Mac next to her at the marble-topped kitchen island, though, his green eyes grew stormy...furious. She was glad she'd never gone against him in battle or anywhere else. "You might be the whiz billionaire CEO of a high-tech manufacturing company, but if you can't see that your sister has grown into a true lady with more kindness and class than all the other society women and photographers combined, you're still an idiot in my book, and she doesn't have to sit here and listen to you make her feel small."

When he pressed the button to end the call, cutting off whatever Drew was just starting to say, Lana's mouth fell open in horrified surprise, then unwilling amusement.

"Oh my God! You just hung up on my brother."

Mac's smile was lopsided. "I surely did," he confirmed. "I think maybe it's something you should do more often."

"But…but…*nobody* talks that way to Drew. He's kind of, I mean, isn't he like your boss?" she asked, suddenly worried he'd just lost his job over her.

"Nah, Pat's my boss, and I'm on leave, anyway." Mac shrugged. "Even if Drew were my boss, though, it'd be worth it. I can't believe that's how he speaks to you…treats you. Has it always been like that between you two?"

Deep in thought, Lana sat down on one of the tall metal stools and pushed the nearly forgotten lemonade over to Mac. "I guess so? Some of the way he treats me is well-earned. I was…pretty lost after our parents died." She gave a hollow laugh. "Not that things were so great when they were alive, either. Drew and Fitz — although Fitz to a lesser extent because he was younger — always kind of had to parent me. I could be an all-out brat at home as a little girl, desperately trying to get any attention from our parents. I wish someone would have told me that you can't squeeze blood from a stone."

She pictured her parents as she'd seen them as a child — her father, tall and handsome, always drinking and laughing, surrounded by friends, devilishly charismatic, and her mother, willowy, glamorous and so beautiful it hurt to look at her...but remote...brittle. Lana hadn't even been allowed to touch her, for fear she would muss her with sticky hands or too-tight hugs. Together, Bertie and Sabrina Fitzhugh had been something to see, but their relationship had been tumultuous on the best of days, constantly dissolving into blistering arguments, slammed doors and weeping.

Then, one night, they'd just been gone, killed in an instant—and everything had changed.

"I look like my mother, you know. Everyone tells me how beautiful she was and how much I resemble her, as if that's something I should like to hear."

The strong column of Mac's tanned neck worked as he took a swallow of lemonade. "You don't?" he asked.

Lana shook her head, just once, but hard. "*No*," she answered, and the word came out like a missile of sound, harder than she'd intended. "Although when I was a teenager...back then I would have eaten it up, having that connection to such a famous, stunning woman. I wanted that same reputation and popularity for myself, *so* badly, to finally feel like I really, truly belonged."

"I think we all feel that way when we're young," Mac observed. "Hell, it's part of why I joined the Navy...to fit in and have my place in something, an institution my daddy and my granddaddy were part of as well."

It was the perfect opening to contrast her young self with the man Mac had been. Heck, he'd already told her things he wasn't proud of, too. But now that the moment was upon her, Lana found herself still reluctant to reveal how cruel and selfish she'd been.

Mac seemed to feel her hesitation, and he stroked his knuckle along her cheek to draw her attention to him. "Hey, now…you don't have to tell me anythin' else — nothin' you don't want to. I'm not goin' anywhere," he said gently, and she ached for the tenderness she felt from him.

It was that tenderness that gave her the courage to continue. "No," she sucked in a long, deep breath, blowing it out quickly. "I promised."

His expression was patient, his vibrant eyes encouraging her, and she managed a trembling smile before she continued.

"When I was teenager, I did do all those things Drew accused me of. I wore makeup an inch thick, tops held together by strings designed so that my breasts practically popped out of them and skirts so short I could barely walk in them."

"I would like to have seen that," Mac murmured. "In fact, I'd *still* like to see that," he added, raising one eyebrow suggestively.

Lana snorted and rolled her eyes, pressing her lips tightly together to keep from smiling, but the tension had lessened, just as she was sure Mac had intended.

"I'd never had a large number of friends, but I had a couple of closer ones, and of course, my best friend, Sam. Sam never cared what I wore." She felt an ache building in the back of her throat. "However, Sam and I were never remotely what I'd call popular, and I wanted that so desperately." She turned pleading eyes toward Mac, willing him to understand. "I think now that maybe I was equating popularity with a way to get closer to my parents, more specifically to my mother, who I missed in death even more for not having really been close to her when she was alive.

"Sam didn't like to talk about it or spend much time at her house, but from the little time we did spend there, I always got the sense that something wasn't right at home. She never talked about the dynamics, but she...never seemed to trust her family, especially not her distant cousin, Rick. He was awful to her, always teasing her and playing pranks, but not in a childish, oh-he's-a-prankster way. These were downright cruel and deliberate...custom-targeted. Some of them really hurt her." She drew in a shaky breath, forcing herself to keep talking.

"When he transferred to the same private high school we attended, things got even worse. Rick was instantly popular, practically the king of the school overnight, and he used his position to bully Sam until she was a complete pariah. To my everlasting shame, I started sticking up for her less and less." She looked up at Mac again, and his eyes were soft, understanding. She didn't deserve his sympathy, but it felt good, nonetheless. She traced the moisture of the built-up condensation on the outside of her glass as she continued, making swirling patterns.

"One Sunday evening, there was a pool party at Carter Lacey's house — he was probably the next most popular guy — and I got invited, with an extra note saying that Rick had said he really hoped I was coming. I was as thrilled as I was surprised. I rushed to talk to Sam, but...she hadn't been included. She urged me not to go, and finally confessed some things she'd never said before, like that Rick used to hurt her — physically and emotionally — whenever he could get her alone. I wouldn't feel right telling you what, exactly, because it was something she told me in confidence, but...it was awful." Lana could still picture what her friend had looked like that day. Sam's deep blue eyes, so like Gray's, had been filled with sorrow...and genuine worry...for *her*.

"To my everlasting shame, I didn't believe her. It was so outlandish, so at odds with the smooth, handsome boy who everyone at school adored, that I accused her of being jealous, of making everything up in a desperate attempt to keep me unpopular, like she was. We yelled at each other, and I stormed out and went to the party."

She was so agitated she hadn't realized she was shaking until she felt Mac's arms surround her, his warmth chasing away the worst of the memories. "Darlin', you wanna take a break?" he offered. "It's hurtin' me to see you so distraught."

Her hair whipped with how jerky her movements were as she shook her head. "No... If I don't get through it now, I never will, and Mac" — she paused, turning to study his face, only inches from her own — "I really want you to know."

"All right, sugar...then can we sit down so I can hold you, so you can feel how you're not alone?"

She buried her face in his neck, inhaling deeply. He smelled like leaves, grass and sweat, and she'd never felt closer to anyone else. He guided her over to an overstuffed armchair, pulling her down onto his lap and stroking his hand up and down her arm.

Her breath was so deep it made the side of her chest brush against the front of his, just for an instant, before she continued. "The party was just about as bad as you might be imagining...maybe worse. Although I want you to know that I went with Rick willingly, and I didn't say no — at least not to the sex, even though I didn't enjoy it. I suppose I was just so flattered and excited that he wanted me, and I didn't know that it ought to feel good. That part was with my consent. I thought he would be my boyfriend afterward, and we could be like the king and queen of the school." Even though it hurt her to remember, she wanted to be clear on that, because it made what had followed so much worse.

If Mac had spoken, the tears that threatened might have fallen in earnest, so she was grateful he only made a noise of deep understanding.

She braced herself to finish the story. "Well, anyway, him becoming my boyfriend wasn't what happened. He'd been setting me up and had his friends take pictures, which he'd not only sent to our classmates but to the media as well. They weren't X-rated, but they were pretty suggestive. He waited a little bit, but by the time I got to school on Monday morning, he'd told everyone that I was a nymphomaniac who'd begged him to do all sorts of things with me. All those other kids who'd known me for years believed him, so easily, and I just had time to see the disdain on their faces before Drew pulled me out of class. He'd seen the pictures, too—everyone had—and it was quite a scandal for our family's company. I got a blistering lecture and threats of reform school."

"Rick was a sadistic bastard…God, honey, I'm so sorry that happened to you. I can't even imagine," Mac said quietly, but his tone was no less vehement for all that it wasn't loud.

"I convinced Drew that I would change, act better, and he allowed me to stay at the same school, but when I went back…Sam was gone. She'd convinced her great-uncle to send her to boarding school, the same one where our other childhood friend, Cain, went. I ended up changing schools, too." She stared, unseeing, at Mac's face, lost in her memories. "It was just...too hard, constantly dealing with the things everyone said."

"Nobody could blame you, honey. You were just a teenager—and a lonely one. Everybody makes the wrong choice sometimes."

Intellectually, Lana knew that Mac's words were true, but she couldn't fully bring herself to believe them.

"There's more," she whispered, and Mac's frame went taut beneath her.

"I, ah, didn't feel too well after everything, but I just thought I was sore, and I didn't really know what was normal. So, I didn't say anything to anyone for a long time..." She couldn't contain the broken sob that tore out of her chest, but she made herself finish. "By the time I went to the doctor, I had a really advanced infection that had spread everywhere in my pelvis. They were able to treat me with IV antibiotics and fully clear the infection so it's not contagious and won't come back, but...the scarring..." Her voice wavered again. "I can never be a mother," she finished. She hadn't cried about it for a long time—had thought she'd made peace with it—but now she realized she was mourning the future she wished she could have had with Mac, too.

"Is *that* why you pushed me away and keep tellin' me I'm not the kind of man for you?" he asked.

She gulped, swiping at her eyes. "Yes," she managed to croak.

"I'm glad you told me," he answered, and she steeled herself against the disgust she was certain she would see on his face and the way that he would come up with some excuse to leave. At least he'd ensured she and Gray were protected, but she knew that he would distance himself. She expected it, was prepared for it.

"I'm so grateful, honey, that you trusted me with this, because it helps me understand where you're comin' from...and how very badly you've been hurt, by so many people you trusted. But before we talk about that, I want to tell you somethin' important."

Hope was like a wary butterfly in Lana's chest, too afraid to fully unfurl its wings yet. "What?" she asked.

"You're already a parent," he answered gently. "If you don't believe me, ask that little boy upstairs who you completely changed your life to take care of, because he'll tell you somethin' that I understand, too. You don't have to make or carry a child to be a parent. You only need love, which, darlin', you have an abundance of. You practically glow with it, and it's spectacular."

She'd turned to him as he spoke, and the earnestness—along with naked emotion—on Mac's face was undeniable. He believed what he was saying. Her heart thumped, then raced.

"You're not...disgusted? Horrified?" she asked.

He drew his eyebrows together and his eyes were warm with patience and understanding. "*God, no.* I'm not sure there's anything you would or could do to make me feel that way. I see you—the kind of person you are on the inside—and I would be the last person to judge you for some immature decisions you once made." His eyes, so velvet-soft before, were now hardened like polished jewels. "Although I sure as hell *am* gonna blame the people who made you feel so alone, and sad...like you were somehow less...or dirty. Is that asshole, Rick, still around?"

Lana gave a half-shrug. "He kind of disappeared, and I'm not sure what happened to him. I heard a rumor that he was gambling a lot — super fancy, private parties, with high stakes — then I don't know what happened. He wasn't at Sam and Cain's funeral service."

"We'll have to find him, if only so that I can show him what a real man lo—, uh, *caring* for his woman looks like."

Lana's heart did a weird little double-time patter at both the possessiveness she heard in Mac's voice, and the way he had corrected himself. *Was he going to say he loved me?* she wondered.

With a bolt of clarity, the reason she'd been so miserable, knowing that she needed to let Mac go, came into precise focus. She cared for him, as well...*very* deeply. In fact, she was falling in love with him, and had maybe — *probably* — already fallen, just as surely as she had tumbled over the picnic table earlier. More than that, though, he knew the worst of her, and beyond forgiving her, he was *defending* her. Even now, she couldn't see anything other than concern in his expression, along with something softer and infinitely more tender.

Overcome by both relief and the feelings she couldn't believe she'd been so slow to recognize, she impulsively threw her arms around his neck, pressing her lips to his. At first, he was utterly motionless, but it only took an instant for him to respond with flattering eagerness. He deepened the kiss, turning it darker and more passionate. She had the stray thought that he still tasted faintly of lemonade, but then he caressed her tongue with his, pulling her flush against him, and any thoughts other than how good he felt flew out of her mind.

"To be clear, I am in no way complainin', but what was that for?" he asked when they finally broke apart for an instant, barely pulling his lips back so that they tickled hers deliciously as he spoke.

"For being wonderful...for being you and making me feel lighter than I have for years." She scattered kisses on his nose and forehead, and his skin tasted salty. "Maybe ever," she amended.

His frown was exaggerated, and she gave a startled squawk when he lifted her up, resettling her so she was straddling his lap. He rubbed her outer-thighs, exposed by her hiked-up skirt, appreciatively.

"Nope...still the same sexy weight. Perfect." His grin was wolfish.

"You're pretty bold, there, Lieutenant," she scolded him, smiling.

"Ah-ah," he said, shaking his head. "Don't forget Commander. Lieutenant *Commander*. I'm mighty good at commandin'," he drawled, making his accent so syrupy it might as well have been honey.

Her small squirm and the catch in her breath revealed how much the idea excited her, and his eyes widened with interest as he raised his eyebrows.

"Oh my, what's this? Miss Fitzhugh, I do believe you *like* the idea of me takin' control... Is that right, sugar?"

He lifted one hand from her thigh to brush over her breast, unerringly finding her hard nipple even through her sweater and earning a gasp from Lana. His gaze darkened, giving him an appearance that was almost feral...savage.

His voice was husky when he continued. "I think you'd like for me to show you how well I can take care of you by sittin' you down on this chair and holdin' those pretty thighs of yours open so I can taste all your sweet little pussy."

"*Mac*," she moaned, wiggling again on his lap and feeling his rising length growing even harder and longer underneath her.

She wasn't sure who began the kiss this time or whether they simply collided in a mutual explosion of passion, but suddenly he was kissing her like he wanted to devour her. She rocked against him, rubbing shamelessly in an effort to get closer, twining her fingers into his short hair. He felt like he'd been made to fit with her, against her — like two pieces of a puzzle, finally connected.

Mac had just reached both hands up under her top, which she would have happily torn off herself in that moment if only to feel his skin against hers faster, when she heard a faint noise from upstairs. She nearly giggled at how they both went utterly still, like kids in a game of freeze tag, but with his hands cupping her breasts and her skirt up around her waist as she rode his lap.

The noise came again, louder, and this time there was no mistaking the sound.

"Lalaaaaah! La*laaaah*!" Gray was awake from his nap, and he was his usual grumpy, needy post-nap self.

She looked down at Mac, regret filling her entire body until she thought some of it might just spill out of her.

His smile was dry. "Go on... It's okay. Gray needs you." His words were sweet and soft, and he tucked an errant lock of hair behind each of her ears before slowly lifting her off him. "I'll be here," he continued in a voice so low she wasn't certain if he meant her to hear it, but it sounded like a promise.

Leaning over to give him one final, quick, open-mouthed kiss, she whispered, "I'm going to hold you to that, and I can't wait to get you alone again," before she hurried up the stairs to take Gray out of his room.

Chapter Fourteen

At dinnertime the following night, Mac reflected that neither he nor Lana had had any idea that it would take over twenty-four hours for them to be alone together again. *Is this what all parents go through as a couple?* he wondered, then mentally answered his own question. *Of course* all parents went through this, and he needed to hug both of his sisters extra tight the next time he saw them — maybe his brothers-in-law, as well. They all made everything look so easy, when, *man*, it was anything but.

At bedtime the night before, everything had seemed like it was going smoothly, but as soon as Lana had oh-so-carefully pulled Gray's door closed, the soft snick of it latching had woken the preschooler up, and he'd been so fussy and needy that Lana had finally just given up and slept squeezed in like a sardine next to the little boy, in his bed. Then, this afternoon, Gray had again drifted off in his car seat in the SUV, but only during the last five minutes of the trip home from the mall.

Unfortunately, when they'd gotten back to the house and Mac had tried to carry him up to his room, Gray had snapped awake and proceeded to refuse to fall back asleep for any reason.

Now, sitting across the table in his booster seat, Gray was practically nodding off as he slowly chewed and swallowed a green bean. Even as Mac watched, the little boy's chin actually drifted down until he caught himself only a nanosecond before face-planting into the brightly colored, segmented plate.

Mac and Lana exchanged a long look, and her lips twitched, but she didn't make the mistake of mentioning bedtime out loud.

"Gray, baby, would you like to be excused to go play in the other room while we clean up?" she suggested.

His eyes nearly drooping at the corners with sleepiness, Gray nodded. "'Kay, Lala," he mumbled, and almost tripped on his way to the rug that was one of his designated toy areas.

When he was sure Gray was out of earshot, Mac leaned over and whispered conspiratorially, "Do you think we can dare to hope that he might sleep well tonight — or will that jinx us entirely?"

"Uh-oh! You better knock on wood right away and find some salt to throw over your shoulder after tempting fate that way!" Lana scolded him, her eyes dancing.

Holding her gaze intently, Mac rapped the table so gently that it barely made a sound. "You're salty today, darlin'. Can I throw *you* over my shoulder?" he asked, waggling his eyebrows suggestively.

Lana snorted, but her cheeks went pink. "Oh my God, you've been getting more and more outrageous!"

Mac didn't disagree. He'd been stealing touches and making sly comments as often as possible since the day before. "What can I say? I love seein' you blush," he answered, unrepentant.

She flicked one of the cloth napkins toward him. "Have you heard anything more from your buddies?" she asked.

Mac frowned. "Yeah, but there hasn't been any notable activity. I don't like it." He drew his brows together until he felt his forehead crinkle. "Even weirder, we can't seem to get to the end of the money trail for the fortune that Gray is supposed to inherit one day from his mother's family. Gun and his team are still workin' on it, but it's takin' a lot longer than we expected."

He gathered all three dinner plates and carried them to the kitchen, noting that it looked like Gray might have finally just fallen asleep, hunched over a toy firetruck. Mac inclined his chin, indicating to Lana that she should look.

"I think Little Man might have finally run out of gas," he observed.

The lines of Lana's expression were so soft and gentle that he had a hard time remembering how arrogant and unapproachable she'd looked the first time he'd met her, all haughty attitude and designer clothes.

"At the risk of immediate awakening, I have to agree," she answered, crossing her fingers in front of her. When Gray didn't immediately pop back up, they shared a relieved laugh.

"In addition to my guys calling and texting updates, I have also received three calls from your older brother," Mac said.

Lana stopped halfway between sitting and standing. "What? Ugh...I can't *believe* he would call you because he couldn't get me!" she fumed.

Mac's personal opinion was that Drew's calling him had nothing to do with Lana not answering and everything to do with Drew wanting to put him back in his place, but he kept that to himself. The man was Lana's brother, after all, and Fitz's, too, even if he was capable of being a total dick.

"I know you asked me not to speak with him — or Fitz or Pat for that matter — so I won't, but I just wanted you to be aware."

"Thank you," Lana said, and the wattage of her smile could have lit the room better than any lamp. She came to join him at the sink, carrying their drinking glasses.

"So," he asked carefully, trying to be casual as he wiped the first plate with a soapy sponge, "how are you feelin' about yesterday?"

By unspoken agreement, they'd both been avoiding the subject until they could speak without Gray overhearing...or at least, Mac assumed that was why Lana hadn't brought it up.

"Have you changed your mind?" she asked quickly. "If you have — "

Uncaring of the soap suds, Mac covered her cold hands with his warm, sopping ones. "I definitely haven't changed my mind. I'm still honored beyond belief that you trusted me, and I..." He took a deep, fortifying breath. If Lana could be brave enough to bare her own past, Mac could sure as hell be brave enough to tell her how he felt. "I still care about you, even more than I did when we...separated a few months back. I know I told you I dreamed of you, but I also never stopped thinkin' of you, hearin' something funny and wantin' to tell you...never stopped longin' to kiss and hold you again, either. Everything you told me yesterday doesn't change anything about how I feel."

Her eyes were shiny, and she was looking at him as if he'd hung the moon, as his momma would have said.

"I thought of you every day, Mac, and wished things were different. Then, when I was worried and scared, you were the person I most wanted — *needed* — with me. I think..." She bit her lip thoughtfully. "I think that I've been holding on to this idea of myself as damaged and unworthy of being with someone good — anyone I could really care about — for so long that I'm having trouble trusting how you feel, how *I* feel."

Mac searched her expression and saw real fear behind her distinctive blue eyes. His first instinct was to be offended that she didn't trust him, but if he'd learned anything from both the Navy and his long recovery from his injury, it was patience. Lana was worth it. Still, he couldn't let her comment go unanswered.

"I get that, darlin', but let me try to tell you how I see you. You're gorgeous, smart, well-educated and you have a wicked sense of humor. You could have spent your life doin' nothin' but countin' your piles and piles of money — Scrooge McDuck-style — but instead, not only do you work for philanthropic causes, you throw yourself into them wholeheartedly. You work tirelessly and bring real improvements to your community. I love bein' with you, and I can tell already that Gray does, too. I don't care about your past, except to wish you hadn't been hurt so badly by it."

When she started to open her mouth, he stopped her by pressing a gentle kiss to her lips.

"No, honey...I didn't tell you those things to make you answer now. I just wanted you to know, to think about another way to see yourself — how I see you." It felt strange to open himself up, knowing that she was uncertain, but it also felt right.

"I'm gonna quickly finish these dishes then attempt to carry Gray to bed without wakin' him." He stepped closer to her, so that he could smell her shampoo mingled with the faint scent that was distinctly hers, a sweet spiciness that always clung to her skin, driving him slowly mad. If either of them took a deep breath, it would close the gap between their bodies.

"If he stays asleep, I'm hopin' — so damn much — that you'll come join me in my room, in my bed." He couldn't keep the husky note of possession out of his voice. "If you need more time, I'll understand. I told you I'm not goin' anywhere. But be sure about it when you come, because I don't think that I'll be able to let you go a second time, darlin'."

* * * *

Both Lana's mind and body were still reeling, and even after Mac had left the kitchen to carry Gray upstairs, it was almost as if the echoes of his presence still lingered. When he'd told her how he felt, she didn't know how to react. She wanted to trust him, to believe in how he saw her, but the familiar whisper that she was dirty, wrong and unlikable threatened to undermine the luminous joy his words had brought her. It was easy to flirt, to exchange small touches and smiles as they had all day, but tonight — the way he'd laid it all out there — that was much harder.

As she finished wiping the crumbs off the table — mostly concentrated on Gray's side — she knew in her heart that she wanted to find the courage and strength to be just as honest as Mac had been. And oh, there was no question of whether she wanted him. She ached for him with every molecule of her body.

Keeping one ear strained to hear any noise from Gray, she nearly sprinted to her bathroom, hurrying through brushing her teeth and freshening up. When she caught a glimpse of her reflection in the mirror, her cheeks were pink and her eyes sparkled with excitement. Touching her throat, she realized she was nearly breathless with joy, and her heart raced. She was definitely going to Mac's room, and she was thrilled — but along with expectation came a wave of nerves.

When she went back out to her bedroom, she looked around a little wildly. *What am I supposed to wear to a tryst in the bedroom of a man who is going to be my lover…maybe more? How the heck have I made it to twenty-seven years old without having any idea about any of this?* She raised her hand again to the hollow of her throat, as if she could force her pounding heart to slow, and drew in a long, calming breath.

It probably didn't matter what she wore. If she went to his room in a baggy sweatsuit and a ratty bathrobe, she imagined Mac would happily welcome her. *And get me naked*, she acknowledged. She shivered at the thought.

She decided to go with a simple, blush-pink jersey-knit nightgown with spaghetti straps — soft, casual, but hopefully still more alluring than a sweatsuit — and, in a fit of wickedness, left off both bra and panties so she was bare underneath. There still hadn't been any sort of noise from Gray's room, and she registered mingled relief that the coast remained clear and trepidation that nothing was stopping her. Thoughts of watching Mac's slow smile, hearing the sensual words he'd speak to her in his smooth drawl, were enough to force her feet to move. She wanted this for herself, but even more, she wanted this for Mac…to give herself to him.

When she carefully turned his doorknob, mindful of trying to be quiet, and pushed the heavy door, her hands felt strange, almost unsteady. Then the door opened the rest of the way, tugged from the other side, and Mac was pulling her into the room and his arms as if he couldn't keep his hands off her and everything was all right…better than all right.

"You came," he breathed against her hair, running his hands in long strokes up and down her back. "I wasn't sure if you would. Mm-m, darlin', you look so gorgeous, *feel* so gorgeous." He took a deep sniff. "Smell gorgeous, too," he added.

His words, and the way he was touching her, a combination of reverent and sensual, made her feel like the most beautiful woman in creation.

"I'm not sure anything could have kept me away," she confessed.

Mac pushed her back against the door, which snicked closed behind her, caging her with his arms on either side of her head so that his handsome face was only inches from hers. "I feel it, too…like we're magnets, powerful ones, just achin' to fit together."

His description was so apt and sexy that her breath hitched.

"I'd like to take a moment to properly appreciate this outfit you're wearin', but I'm not sure I can keep my hands off you for that long," he continued, and she saw out of the corners of her eyes that his fingers were twitching, as if they might go rogue from the rest of his body and start touching her again on their own.

There was only one small lamp lit in the room, and it bathed the space in mellow, golden light, gilding his hair, eyebrows and the trace of his five o'clock shadow, along with the hairs on his muscular forearms. Mac's expression was everything Lana could have wished to see, sensual and adoring, with a hint of wild desperation threatening to break through.

"Don't keep your hands off me, then," she invited. She wasn't sure where the throaty vixen's voice had come from, but she wasn't sorry.

It was all the encouragement Mac needed as he bent his head to slant his mouth over hers, pressing their bodies together against the door so fast that the movement made a muffled thump. His taste, faintly minty and darkly sensual, teased her mouth as she opened to him, and he deepened the kiss immediately, rocking against her as he smoothed caresses first along her sides, then reaching around to cup the fullness of her butt.

Lana moaned against his mouth, shifting to push more firmly into his hands, a movement which thrust her chest out as well so that her full breasts rubbed tantalizingly against his hard chest.

"Aw, that's right, honey… You feel so good," he encouraged with low murmurs, kneading the globes of her ass with his fingers, even as he shifted rhythmically to rub against her tightened nipples and work his growing hardness against her. It was a sensual onslaught, and she was helpless to do anything other than give herself over, holding on to Mac's broad shoulders and opening herself more fully as she lifted one leg up to wrap around him.

She felt him stiffen for a second when she touched his prosthetic leg with her calf. "Don't stop...Mac. It's so wonderful," she gasped the encouragement, and he started to move again.

"Need to feel you better, darlin'," he rasped, and that was all the warning she had before he gripped the hem of her nightgown and pulled it up and totally off.

"Mm-m...such a good girl, leaving yourself soft and bare underneath for your man," he growled, and something inside of her basked in heady pleasure at his praise.

"For you," she whispered, whimpering as he bent his head to suck one of her pink nipples into the heat of his mouth. The dual sensations of the cold wood of the door against her back, combined with the heat of Mac at her front, made her shiver with awareness...and intense arousal.

As he licked and tugged at the bud with his mouth, she threw her head back against the door with a low sigh of pleasure. "Oh, Mac, that's so good," she murmured, caressing his short-cropped hair and holding him against her before she realized what she was doing.

He let her first nipple go with an audible pop. "Gonna make you feel even better, sugar...gonna take you so high, make you so wet you'll be drippin' before I fill you with my cock."

He bent to take her other nipple into his mouth, and the feeling of him sucking, along with the vivid images his filthy words had conjured, had her thrashing against him with helpless abandon.

He chuckled, the vibration of the sound against her tightened peak making her gasp.

"You're so sensitive, sugar, so fuckin' responsive. It's hot as hell."

Her answer was to pull at the hem of his thin, cotton shirt, which he practically tore off in answer to her silent request. When she felt the slide of the bare skin of their chests together, her core went liquid with arousal.

"Mac, yes, God, yes," she encouraged, not totally sure what she was encouraging but totally on board.

He chuckled again as he reached a hand between them, kissing all over her chest and neck as he did. "I bet...I'm gonna...feel you...gettin' so wet...for me." His voice came out in time with his kisses, and she pushed into his hand when he cupped her mound and stroked one sure finger with aching gentleness into her delicate folds.

"So wet," she agreed, hiking her leg up higher on his lean hip to give him better access.

"Oh yeah," he answered with dark satisfaction, adding a second finger and stroking up and down the length of her slit before circling around the bundle of nerves that had grown so incredibly sensitive, yearning for his touch. "Are you gonna let me taste some of that sweet honey you're makin'?"

She froze at his suggestion. "It's okay... You don't..."

Mac lifted his head and caught her gaze, observing her until she wanted to squirm. The sudden comprehension she saw register in his expression made her feel even more naked than she already was.

"Wait! Honey, have you...? Has nobody ever done that with you?"

She felt awkward, gauche and shifted slightly, but with Mac's hand still between her legs, the small movement made her bite back a moan of pleasure at the sensation.

She shook her head, biting her lip. "I...with any other guys I dated, I always pulled back before we got to any of this part. I just didn't really feel it."

Mac's eyes widened. "Wait, Lana! Are you sayin' that you haven't made love to anyone since that asshole when you were a teenager?"

Now she just wanted to curl into a lump on the floor. Still, this was *Mac*, and he deserved an answer, even if it would probably make him reconsider. "Yeah," she said in a small voice. "There hasn't been anyone else."

She'd thought Mac might step away, but instead, the oddest expression flittered across his face and into his eyes...like horror mixed with deep masculine satisfaction.

"Darlin', you're honorin' me more than I can ever say by givin' this to me, and I can't wait to show you how good things can be between a man and woman...between me and you." His voice was deep and gravelly, and all the arousal that had fled with her awkwardness returned in full force at the heat in his voice and expression.

Chapter Fifteen

Mac hated how much he enjoyed knowing that his gorgeous, sensuous Lana was essentially inexperienced and that he would get to be the first to show her real pleasure. She'd never even had a man go down on her... His cock stirred and twitched at the thought. The wave of primal possessiveness that rose, hard and fast, startled him with its intensity.

He lowered his head, capturing her lips again, teasing and tasting, then stroking into her mouth until she was mewling and moaning with pleasure once more, arching against him. "You're mine," he growled, the thought coming out of his mouth without him meaning to speak the words.

Lana's deep blue eyes went soft and yielding, though, warm with arousal. "Yours," she sighed, but he heard it, and it made his cock feel like it might explode with how much harder it grew, almost impossibly so. It seemed that his woman liked knowing who she belonged to.

He went back to kissing her mindless, starting with her lips, then moving to her neck, ears and breasts. When he broke off their kiss again, the sound of her panting—loud in the quiet room—made deep satisfaction flare in his chest.

"Come lie down on the bed, darlin', and let me show you how good it will feel for me to lick your sweet little pussy," he said, his tone husky with need.

Her only answer was a jerky nod, but it was enough, and he guided her to the bed with one large hand on the small of her back. He couldn't help but admire the bounce of the full globes of her ass as she took the few steps to cross the room.

He gave a strangled groan of appreciation when he saw the little flower on the lower left-hand side of her back, which he was surprised he hadn't seen before if her shirt hiked up. "There it is... I was wondering when I was gonna see your body picture," he teased, using the same words Gray had for his tattoo. "It's adorable," he commented, imagining how he could kiss it later. In fact, he might just want to kiss it every day. He loved that idea.

She blushed and made a gorgeous picture, looking back over her shoulder at it. "Part of my wild teenage years. Because it's on my back, I sometimes forget it's even there."

"Well, now, I'm happy to remind you that I like all the parts of you whenever you want...but most of all, I like the way they're put together." He gave her a mock leer—or maybe just a real leer, since damn, she looked amazing naked—and she flushed pink as she laughingly turned to look forward again, taking the final few steps.

Her confidence seemed to falter a little, and she hesitated when they got right to the edge of the large bed, as if she weren't sure what to do. Now that he knew about her relative inexperience—and that what little experience she did have hadn't been very good—many of her actions and reactions made a lot more sense.

"I want to see you lying down with your thighs open and that pretty pussy pink and glistenin' for me." It was a sensual command, and he punctuated it by using his hand, still touching right above her spectacular ass, to give her just enough of a push that she toppled forward onto the bed.

The sound she made was close to an incensed squawk, and when she turned, she looked up at him from an irate face, surrounded by her silky hair, tousled haphazardly by his fingers earlier. "Hey!" she complained.

"You were too slow," he returned. He kept his tone light, but he wasn't sure he was teasing…wasn't sure if he was capable of it at the moment. The desperation to touch her again, to taste her, was like a living thing deep inside him.

Her eyes sparked with answering heat.

"Oh, God, baby…you're fuckin' perfect. Come over here and let your legs dangle over the edge of the bed," he ordered, and she shimmied down the silky quilt to where he stood.

He wanted nothing more than to kneel, but to his horror, he realized that it wasn't going to be like he remembered, being able to kneel and worship a woman before his injury. *Why the hell didn't I think of this before I put myself in this position?* an angry voice echoed in his head. Just as quickly, he mentally answered his own criticism. *Because I was so caught up in how fucking amazing Lana feels that I forgot...I fucking forgot that I don't have part of my leg anymore.* It was such an amazing, freeing realization that he almost wanted to whoop with joy, but then the reality of it, that he was now either going to have to awkwardly get down onto his knees — which he knew he was lucky to still be able to do, given that many guys with similar injuries had to have amputations above the knee — or he was going to have to backpedal, but Lana would know.

"Mac?" she asked softly, and he could see from her expression that she'd already guessed anyway — or she'd at least guessed something close to the truth. "I think you're sexy..." The sound she made in the back of her throat was so sensual that he practically quivered with need as she continued. "God, so sexy...just as you are now. I wouldn't change anything...well, except the pain that you had to endure. But your injury, your leg and foot being prosthetic...? You earned those, doing your job and saving lots of other soldiers — good men who are alive today because of you. It makes you who you are, and that's the man I'm dying to be with...who turns me on so much I can barely form coherent thoughts."

Mac chuckled wryly. "You seem pretty coherent right now, sugar," he observed dryly.

Lana, naked and tempting in shades of peach, gold and pink where she lay on the bed, had the audacity to laugh. "Well, you know what I meant. But seriously, Mac... Whatever you do, however you get there, I know I'm going to like it, because it'll be with you, so don't worry."

It was sweet and sexy and so entirely Lana that if he hadn't already given her his heart, he would have handed it over right then on a platter. It was also exactly what he'd needed to hear. Lana was the first woman he'd been with since his injury and recovery and, if he had anything to say about it, she'd be the last as well. He could find it in himself to look a little unsteady as he got down to the ground when the reward was the taste of his woman's nectar.

"Is that right? You're sure you're gonna like everythin'?" he asked, bracing his hand on the edge of the bed so he could keep his balance as he knelt. He knew he should be grateful, and he truly was, because it was much easier for him than a lot of the other guys he'd met in the hospital. A big part of the challenge for him was because his injury had totally changed his center of gravity and seriously messed with his equilibrium...but at least he'd been able to keep the knee itself.

When he got down to the floor, he could barely spare a thought for his equilibrium or balance since the position put him at eye-level with Lana's gorgeous pussy and the golden-fleece tuft of hair that covered her mound. His mouth went dry, and when she tentatively started to open her thighs — for him, he knew, because he'd asked her to — he couldn't take his eyes off her.

"That's it, darlin', just like that. Open up for your man," he rumbled, and she let her thighs fall open to reveal her folds, pink and glistening from his earlier attention.

With a growl, he pounced on her, holding her as he covered her cunt with his mouth. Her taste, sweet and tangy, exploded onto his tongue, and he'd never tasted anything better.

"Oh...oh!" she gasped with surprise and pleasure, her cries deepening as he licked up and down the length of her then circled around her button of nerves, listening to see what made her sound the wildest. She strained her legs against his hands, and when he moved one of them so he could press a finger into her hot channel, she squeezed all around his finger, rippling around it as he pushed in and out in rhythmic strokes. He gave a muffled grunt of satisfaction at her response and at how sexy it was to know what she would feel like milking his cock.

When her cries increased in volume, he added a second finger, curling them up until Lana went absolutely wild, bucking up against his mouth and hand. He was relentless, knowing she was close to finding her pleasure, and when she stiffened, her pussy going tight, he exulted in the sensation of her coming apart around him, rippling around his fingers and gasping with helpless pleasure...ecstasy. He drew out her orgasm for as long as he could until she lay limp and spent. Her sweet honey still trickled onto his tongue, and his cock throbbed with raw need, but he was determined to be patient for her.

"Oh my God, Mac...oh my *God*," she repeated, the sound of her breath sawing in and out of her lungs loud in the quiet bedroom.

"Good?" he asked, feeling pride and satisfaction at how well-loved she looked when he straightened to see her, splayed out before him like a sensual feast.

"The best... I never imagined... Oh my *God*," she answered, still out of breath.

Mac's chuckle was amused, with an edge of absolute carnality. "I like that you keep saying that...and there's even more to come, darlin'."

"Mm-m, yes," she sighed dreamily, and it was like she'd stroked his cock with the eagerness of the sound.

With a strangled groan of pure heat, he levered himself to stand again. Lana pushed herself up onto her elbows, making her full breasts wobble enticingly, the tips of her nipples looking extra rosy from his earlier attention.

He felt another flash of discomfort at the idea of revealing himself to Lana, scars and all, in the light of the lamp, but he steeled himself against those doubts. She'd told him she wanted him just this way, and he would show her the respect of believing her. He unfastened and pulled down his dark pants, along with his boxer-briefs, stepping out of the left leg first but then bracing himself again to ease them over his prosthesis, which could catch if he wasn't careful. When he'd kicked his pants to the side, he stood totally naked in front of her.

Mac knew he should force himself to look at Lana's face, to see her reaction to his lower half. He was aware of what his body looked like now and that she'd already seen him put on his prosthesis the other morning, but there were a lot more scars that she hadn't seen, snaking up to his hip, where they'd had to stitch him back together. He was revealing everything to her now. He balled his hands into fists and raised his eyes.

His relief was palpable when he didn't find any trace of what he'd most feared, disgust and pity. Instead, the look on her face was a mixture of tenderness, sympathy, and heat—lots of heat—and as she trailed her gaze up and down his body appreciatively, he fought the urge to preen. When her perusal stopped and rested on his groin, his cock rose, long and thick, proudly pointing toward her. As her mouth dropped open, just a little, he felt a bead of pre-cum escape from the tip.

"You're beautiful," she breathed, and he couldn't doubt her sincerity. "And so…big," she finished, her tone a mixture of a flattering amount of awe and a less-flattering amount of concern. She bit her lip, and he felt the cooling of another bead of pre-cum on his tip. "Are you…are you sure that will fit inside me?"

He gave a strangled laugh. "God, sugar, you're killin' me with how hot and innocent you are." He fisted his cock as he looked at her, reclining on the bed like a pagan fertility goddess, all rounded curves and elegant lines. "It will fit…I'm sure. But I promise to go slow…to make sure it feels good for it to be so big inside you."

She drew a shuddering breath, and Mac noticed that her nether curls were still glistening with moisture in the lamplight.

"Please tell me you're ready…that you want me as badly as I want you," he groaned, not knowing how he would force himself to stop if she had changed her mind but determined to give her the chance.

She slid back on the bed, making room for him, and her eyes were like the blue of a gas flame, hot and brilliant. "I want you, Mac," she whispered.

Her words seemed to unleash something inside of Mac and he came down on top of her, pressing her into the bed with deep, passionate kisses and caresses that had a wild edge…desperate.

"God, Lana…you feel so good…your skin is like satin," he breathed between kisses. He nipped her collarbone, then her earlobe, and she shivered, clutching at him with her legs as he stroked his hardness along and into her moisture without entering her, rubbing his cock against her clit over and over again until she was panting with need and he was coated with her juices. "I'm gonna push inside now...put all of my cock deep into your tight little pussy," he said, his voice rough with desire. He positioned himself at her entrance, then stilled. "Aw, damn...I don't think I have a condom. I, ah, packed in hurry, and I haven't needed them...shit." A brick-red flush touched his cheekbones, and he sounded apologetic.

When he would have put distance between them, she pulled him back firmly. "I know that I'm clean and, well, you know..."

The unspoken reminder that she couldn't have children hung between them, but Lana found that with Mac in her arms, looking at her as though he wanted to both worship and devour her, it didn't sting as much as it had even a few days before.

"I'm clean, too, darlin'. They tested me for just about everythin' when I was in the hospital, and I haven't been with anyone since...but are you sure?" he asked, looking at her intently.

Pressed against the lines of his hard body, surrounded by his spicy scent, Lana had never been more sure of anything. "I trust you, Mac. I'm certain. I want you to come inside me...to fill me up," she said in a low, husky voice.

"You're amazin'... God, Lana, what you do to me," he groaned, fitting the head of his cock at her opening. She was so wet that it made a little squelching noise and she was embarrassed, but his answering smile was feral. "Don't worry about that noise. It sounds fuckin' sexy to me, knowin' how you're drippin' for me. Nothing we ever do between us is wrong, sugar."

His words were raw, primal and she felt her nipples tighten against his chest as her core clenched in renewed arousal. Mac slowly started to push inside her, and she felt herself stretch, nearly to the point of discomfort, but he moved with aching deliberation, frequently checking her expression. She could tell it was an effort by how taut and well-defined the muscles of his arms and shoulders had become, and a sheen of sweat beaded on his forehead.

"I'm about halfway in. How does that feel, baby?" he asked, his voice strained.

"Full...really full, but..." She paused, thinking about it and clenching so that he let out a hiss. "It feels kind of good, too."

Mac's smile was wry. "That's a start, but I think I need to do better than 'kind of good'." Then, she felt the world tipped upside down for a moment as he switched their positions effortlessly, astonishing her with his strength. She was still half-impaled by his length, but now she was on top, in control.

"Mm-m...I like this view," he murmured, and she flushed at the way he was looking at her breasts. "C'mon and bring those tight pink nipples down here so I can suck on them some more," he added, licking his lips, and her channel clenched around him at the sensual command.

She bent forward just a little, still slightly tense in the new position, but the feel of his ravenous mouth sucking and biting her sensitive nipples soon had her writhing against him again. Without meaning to, she realized she was sinking farther down onto his hard length until he was fully seated inside of her, and she felt nothing but delicious fullness.

"Oh...oh...Mac," she sighed in wonderment. "It feels...*mm-m*."

"*Mm-m* for me, too, darlin'," he answered, and she knew he'd understood her incoherent words.

She moved her hips experimentally, earning a gasp from both of them. "Is that...all right?" she asked.

"You do whatever feels good to you, baby. It's all gonna feel amazin' to me," he reassured her, and she rose again, coming down harder this time on a moan that he echoed. She soon set a rhythm that felt incredible, and his cock was so long and thick that he dragged along every sensitive place inside her channel as she clenched around him and he continued to play with her breasts. When she started to pant and squirm, building toward something just out of reach, Mac reached down to stroke her clit gently, and the added sensation made her tumble headlong over the edge into pure ecstasy. He continued pumping his hips below her, and stroking her with just the lightest touch, to draw out her pleasure until she felt like a shuddering, quivering mass of bliss.

When he flipped them so she was beneath him again, she was worried she might be too wrung out to respond...but as soon as he started to move inside of her, she found out how wrong she'd been. The lust that had just been satisfied by a mind-blowing orgasm rushed back, right along with the feel of his swollen length pushing deep inside of her at a new angle.

She wasn't sure if the sound she made was a keening cry or a whimper, but Mac's eyes gleamed with satisfaction.

"You like that, don't you, sugar? Feelin' your man so deep inside you...feelin' me make you mine." He punctuated his words with hard thrusts, and she could only hold on, making incoherent sounds of need.

"I wanted to last longer, but you're so sexy…so fuckin' perfect… I'm gonna come soon…gonna fill you up so you know who you belong to."

The combination of his cock, driving into and out of her in hard strokes, along with how sexy his words were, and the growly possessiveness of them that got to her like nothing else, brought Lana right back to the edge of pleasure.

"Mac!" she wailed. "Please…please!" she begged, not even sure what she was begging for, only that she *needed* it.

He sped up his thrusts, and she felt herself soar again over the cliff and into a freefall of sensation until she felt weightless. He pumped into her three more times before he gave a hoarse yell and his entire body went rigid as he emptied his cock into her, filling her with pulse after pulse of hot seed. He collapsed on top of her, only half rolling off her as an afterthought, so that all his weight wasn't directly on top of her.

Their combined breathing was loud and harsh. Lana realized that she didn't have the air to tell Mac how utterly incredible that had been, even if she could have thought of the best words, which she seriously doubted, since every brain cell had suddenly taken a backseat to pure sensuality. When she finally managed to turn her head, she found that Mac's face was only about an inch away from hers, and his soft expression of total contentment exactly matched how she felt.

"So that's what a real man caring for his woman looks like, hm?" she finally managed to say, echoing his words from two days earlier.

Mac was so close to her that his huff of laughter made all the little wispy hairs blow around her sweat-dampened face, and she could see every tiny crinkle around his eyes and mouth.

"That is *exactly* what it looks like, darlin', although I hope to God that we didn't have an audience. I haven't heard a peep from Gray's room, for which I'm thankful, since you were loud enough to wake the dead." He softened the statement with a quick peck on the tip of her nose.

She felt heat rise into her cheeks, then all over her face, and knew she must be blushing as brightly as a tomato. "I was...overcome," she said defensively.

"And I don't think I've ever seen anythin' more beautiful that watching you be overcome...three times, was it?" His tone was tender, but with a hint of smugness. She was perfectly happy to let him be smug, though. He'd more than earned it.

"Yes," she confirmed, smiling shyly. "I...really never imagined it could be like that," she confessed.

Mac shifted so that he could put his arm around her, and her head was pillowed on his chest, right over his extremely prominent eagle tattoo. "I'm so angry at that asshole from your past, but so very glad that I got to show you how good it could be—and it was phenomenal."

She wanted to keep talking but, totally sated, cuddled against his chest and with his heartbeat a steady thrum against her cheek, she felt her eyelids growing heavier in spite of herself.

"Mm-hmm," she echoed, and Mac's chuckle was indulgent.

"Good night, darlin'...sweet dreams," he murmured, and she fell into a deep, blissful sleep, feeling safe and protected.

Chapter Sixteen

Some sort of faint noise woke Mac, and he could tell from the dim quality of the sunlight that it was still pretty early in the morning. In spite of the early hour, he felt amazing. It took him only an instant to realize why, when he looked down to see Lana's golden-blond hair spilling over his chest where she still slept. After she'd fallen asleep—and he had another moment of self-satisfaction at how damn well-loved she'd looked—he'd only crept out of bed to crack the door open so they'd be sure to hear any noise that Gray made overnight. Then he'd slipped back under the blankets, next to her, and she'd curled right back into his side as if he'd never left.

She was just as lovely by the early-morning light as she had been by the lamp light the night before, and he took an extra second to appreciate the elegant curve of her cheek and lips. He was so far gone, he even liked the shape of her ear, for God's sake.

The slight sound came again, and even though he'd only been staying with Lana and Gray for a few days, he recognized that Gray was starting to wake up. The preschooler wasn't fully there yet, but he would be soon. Mac hated to wake her, but he knew Lana would want as much warning as possible. Also—and he valued his life too much to say this to her face—he suspected that his Lana was not really a morning person, since she tended to be slow to stir and get moving...and somewhat grouchy.

He stroked his fingertip down her bare arm, and she barely twitched, so he shook her gently. "Lana, darlin'," he murmured.

She cracked one eye open, just a sliver, and answered in a voice still heavy with sleep, sounding confused. "Mac? What is it?"

His heart nearly turned over in his chest when she burrowed into his side more deeply, and another part of his body came to instant attention as well at the feel of her lush curves pressed all along his side.

"Sugar, I can hear Gray startin' to move around. It's still early, and I'm happy to go tend to him, but I thought you'd probably want to."

At the mention of Gray's name, Lana made a visible effort to rouse herself, and she lifted her head to look at him. "Sorry," she mumbled. "I'm so sleepy...haven't slept so well in..." She paused. "Well, I don't remember ever sleeping that well before."

Mac didn't even try to stop the self-satisfied grin that spread across his face. "I hope to keep you sleepin' well by tuckin' you in the same way every night for the next long while, then." He spoke lightly, without thinking, and a cold lump of ice lodged in his chest at how stricken and worried she looked.

"Mac, I'm not really sure..." she said cautiously, and with sickening clarity, he suddenly understood how the several women he'd had brief relationships in the couple of years after his engagement and before his injury had felt when he'd broken things off with them.

"Forget I said that. I was movin' too fast...lookin' ahead too far." He rushed to speak before she could continue, not wanting to hear exactly what she was going to say. He knew she was skittish and had been hurt badly in the past. He'd been caught up in the beauty of what they'd shared, and it might have meant more to him than it had to her, or maybe she wasn't yet willing to commit to what it had meant. Whatever she intended to say right now, unless she was planning on kicking him out, wasn't going to change how he felt, since he was now sure that he loved Lana...loved her so much it felt bigger than both of them. That kind of love could keep being patient.

"It isn't that I don't think we'll get there. It's just... I'm not..." Lana was obviously uncomfortable, pulling the sheet up to cover her stunning breasts — which was a pity — and Mac cursed himself silently for spooking her.

He brushed his knuckle over the creamy skin of her cheek and held her gaze, trying to hide how much her reluctance had hurt him. It was just a knee-jerk reaction, and he could be reasonable.

"Lana, it's okay. Truly," he said reassuringly. The silence between them was thick, though, and not as comfortable as it had been.

Gray chose that moment to come to full wakefulness with a gusty yell for Lana, but she hesitated for a second.

"It's fine, honey. Go take care of Gray," he urged. "We can talk when you're more comfortable, if you still want to." He picked up her nightgown from where he had ended up flinging it onto the chair near the bed — and he thought that pale pink might just have become his favorite color after the way she'd look in it in the night before — and handed it to her silently.

When Gray yelled again, the look in her eyes grew resigned. "All right...and I'm sorry. I'm just... It's a lot," she admitted.

Mac got it. He really did. He just needed a moment to get over his instinctive hurt before he could be reasonable again.

Lana slid the nightgown over her head before heading toward Gray's room, and Mac lay back on the bed with a sigh. He picked up his phone almost as a reflex, checking the security feeds and logs. Still nothing. The lack of any sort of attempt at entry, after such a concentrated previous period, bothered him even more today than it had yesterday.

As he was looking at his phone, another notice popped up, this time a text from Gun.

Called in a favor at the courthouse to look through docs before they open, but filing system is crap. Will take a while to look through bunch.

Mac texted back before even really considering what he was typing.

Need 2nd set of eyes?

After he'd hit the button to Send, though, he realized it was the perfect chance to get just a little bit of distance and calm. Plus, he was itching to do more to keep Lana and Gray safe, and if that more ended up being research, he was game.

Lana and Gray should be totally protected here at the house alone for only a couple of hours, especially since there hadn't been any recent activity. Mac hoped that the unidentified person or people had given up — but with all the effort they'd already put into their crazy plan, it seemed more likely they were just regrouping.

Gun's reply came back almost immediately, along with the address and room number of the file room where he was.

Sure.

Mac shot back, *Be there soon*, and concentrated on getting ready with quick efficiency so he was passing by Gray's room only a couple of minutes later.

"Good morning, buddy," Mac said brightly to Gray.

"Good morning!" Gray answered, currently in the process of trying to shove two legs into the same leg opening of his pants, and totally undeterred by the impossibility of it.

"All is quiet with the system, and apparently on all fronts, but Gun needs some STAT help with research, so I'm headed downtown." Mac checked the time on his phone. "I think we have to finish by nine, so I should only be gone an hour or two, tops. Will you guys be okay?"

A frown marred Lana's beautiful face, and she looked like she felt guilty, which made him feel worse. He could tell that it was an effort for her to sound cheerful, and he thought maybe she might want a short break from him as well.

"Absolutely," she confirmed. "Gray and I will arm the alarm after you leave, and we won't even go outside while you're gone."

"Perfect... That's exactly what I wanted to hear. If anything comes up, I'll have my phone on me, and you can also just press the panic button to call one of Gun's crew, and whoever's the closest will come immediately." He went into the room to ruffle Gray's bright tangle of curls. "I really can't imagine what could possibly come up in a couple of hours with you stayin' inside, though."

Lana nodded, and she sounded deliberately hearty. "Totally agree... We'll be great!"

Is she truly that eager I'm leaving? popped into Mac's head, but he dismissed the thought immediately. *He'd* made things awkward. They'd be better when he got back. He'd see to it.

"Well, all right, then. See you soon!" he answered. He almost didn't kiss her, but he couldn't help himself, and her lips were soft and yielding under his in the too-brief embrace. Maybe she wasn't as upset with him as he'd thought.

* * * *

After Mac left, while she and Gray made a simple breakfast of egg bites and toast, which was quick to eat and clean up after, Lana spent the first half-hour berating herself. The morning had started off as pure perfection. Mac had said something sweet, and her insecurities had caused her to shut him down and make things weird. He'd tried to mask it, but she'd seen the naked hurt on his face, which he'd promptly hidden.

She just couldn't believe, after telling herself for the past twelve years that no truly good man would want to be with her if she told him about her past, that Mac genuinely wanted to pursue a long-term relationship with her. She couldn't help but think that, once the newness wore off, he would realize she was damaged with a bad reputation and couldn't give him biological children of his own. If she gave herself to him fully, heart and soul, as she longed to...if he ended things then, she thought it might destroy the little kernel of hope she'd managed to protect all these years.

When she thought about it—really thought about it—she knew that her fears were probably way off base. Mac had shared his past with her and trusted her not to judge him too harshly for something he'd once done and had changed since doing. Unfortunately, fear and the memories of past trauma weren't logical, though. She vowed that, starting as soon as he got back from his mysterious research errand, she would try to be more open with Mac—and to communicate. They both seemed to want to suppress their own feelings to make the other person feel better, and while their impulses were admirable, it certainly wasn't the best way to go about building a relationship.

She was so deep in her own thoughts, only half-listening to Gray's chatter as he played with giant plastic blocks and cars, that the sound of the doorbell nearly made her jump out of her skin. She checked her phone, pulling up the app for the new security system, and saw Mrs. Schultz beaming and waving at the security camera, carrying several bags. Lana did the math and realized the long-time housekeeper was back from her leave several days early, but as soon as the idea of Mrs. Schultz as a possible conspirator in a plot to harm Gray or fool Lana into thinking she was going crazy crossed Lana's mind, she dismissed it as ridiculous. She'd known the older woman since she'd been a child, and Sam had trusted her completely. Whoever was behind this, it wasn't Mrs. Schultz.

However, Lana reasoned, if for some reason Mrs. Schultz decided to tackle her to the ground when she opened the door, she'd keep her finger on the panic button on her cell phone, and there were other similar buttons in all the alarms around the house. It was odd that none of Gun's men had given her a heads-up that someone was approaching, she thought, but then she figured that they must have to take breaks sometime. She wasn't going to get bent out of shape about someone happening to take a break during the five minutes that something exciting actually took place at the house after the past few days of total quiet.

"Gray, baby, can you wait here at the table while I go get the door? And don't come follow me until I say so, all right?" Lana knew she was probably being overly cautious, but everything that had happened recently had really spooked her.

"Okay, Lala!" he answered, and she gave it about half-and-half odds that he'd listen, but she knew he had the best intentions.

When she pulled the door open for Mrs. Shultz, she was engulfed in a familiar wave of the mélange of a drugstore perfume that had been popular about forty years earlier—which was probably when the older woman had started wearing it—along with vanilla and cinnamon. As always, it took Lana right back to hugs from the older housekeeper when she'd been a child, on outings with Sam or on the rare occasions they'd gone to Sam's house. After the funerals, everything had been so unsettled, and if she'd smelled the scent on Mrs. Schultz then it hadn't registered, but it sure took her back now...so that her eyes stung for a second.

"Oh, Lana, it's so good to see you! And with such a fancy new security system, too!" Mrs. Schultz enthused. She leaned forward, as if anyone else might be there to overhear. "I'm happy to see that, you know, since the other one seemed to have been acting strangely sometimes. With everything that happened, I don't know if I mentioned it — not the most important thing at a time of such sorrow, you know? — but I think Samantha was intending to replace it herself."

Lana's ears practically twitched she was listening so hard. "She was? How interesting... Yes, we did seem to be having some issues with the system." She tried to act casual, but thought she might have failed. "Weren't you planning to be back next week?" she asked.

Mrs. Schultz looked nonplussed for a second, then sheepish. "Oh, Lana, I'm so sorry! My mind has been scattered lately, what with my husband having unexpected complications after his surgery. He's feeling much better, and the doctor even cleared him for an increase in light activities, so Emily — you remember my daughter? — she came from Michigan to help out, so I thought I'd come back early, but I completely forgot to tell you."

The older woman's face creased with apology, and Lana waved away her concerns. "That's great news! I'm so happy to hear it, Mrs. Schultz, and of course it's not a problem for you to come back earlier. No need to call! We can definitely use your help. My friend,

Lieutenant Commander Joe MacKenzie, is staying here with us right now, too."

Mrs. Schultz nodded knowingly. "Men are wonderful in so many ways, but I have found that they easily make twice or three times the mess of any woman. I can only imagine!" She pursed her lips, as if picturing the mountains of trash and laundry that Mac might have brought with him. "Although, of course, I'm delighted to hear that you and Grayson have a guest. Quite lovely," she added, sounding like she felt she ought to, and Lana had to stifle a giggle.

"Come on in!" Lana invited, widening the door and eyeing Mrs. Schultz's multiple bags. "I can ask Mac — that's what Gray and I call Lieutenant Commander MacKenzie — to program you into the system when he gets back from running out to take care of something. Can I help you with your bags?"

Mrs. Schultz's eyes widened as if she were shocked at the very idea. "I would never let the lady of the house, nor a guest, carry my bags for me!" she sputtered. "I do apologize for the, *erm*, volume of them, but Emily wanted to send a few things over for Grayson, in the hopes that they might cheer him up."

"How kind of her," Lana answering, meaning it. She remembered Emily Schultz as being a sweet girl, just a little older than Sam and her.

"I'll just make two trips," Mrs. Schultz said with a decisive nod, and Lana didn't have the heart to insist, knowing how the older housekeeper loved propriety.

As they walked into the house, toward the kitchen, Gray came running over excitedly. "Miz Schultz!" he cried.

Her face creased into a wide, affectionate smile, and Lana suspected that Mrs. Schultz had probably been worried about Gray and that might be part of the reason for her early return, too.

"Are those surprises? For me?" he asked, dancing around the kitchen.

"Not these," Mrs. Schultz answered, turning to put something away in the drawer. "But I do have some gifts in my other bags," she said absently.

"Yay!" Gray cheered. "Can't wait to see!"

"Did you happen to move some of the dishes, dear?" Mrs. Schultz asked Lana.

Lana suddenly felt like she was in elementary school again and had been caught passing a note. "I...well, I certainly might have," she answered.

Mrs. Schultz was silent, but her shoulders were stiff. "Of course, that's absolutely *your* decision, but I have found that the organization system that Samantha favored—which I taught her—is of superior functionality."

"Oh, well, that's fine, then... I was just, you know, cooking for Gray and me, and... But I don't have my heart set on moving them permanently," Lana stammered. She was happy to pick her battles and arguing with Sam's kitchen organization—which clearly meant something to the older housekeeper— did *not* need to be one of them.

"Very good," Mrs. Schultz said with satisfaction, leaning over to take out a few dishes. "I'll get this place back to ship-shape in no time."

Something that had been tickling at the back of Lana's mind since Mrs. Schultz's surprise arrival popped back into her head. "I didn't hear your car," Lana observed.

Mrs. Schultz shook her head, which, given how tightly she knotted her now-gray hair, didn't make it move an inch. "Oh, no, dear. I didn't drive. I left both cars at home for my husband and Emily. I took one of those new-fangled ride-share things. Emily ordered it for me on her telephonic application."

Lana wanted to snort at the way that Mrs. Schultz described a smart phone app, but Mrs. Schultz was already continuing.

"It was so funny… The driver was quite friendly and, while I don't usually notice these things, he was handsome, too, but he reminded me so much of that awful second- or third-cousin of Samantha's that I just couldn't wait to get out of the car. He was probably one of those shameless photographers, too, since he kept staring so intently at the house. I think I'll have to ask Emily to come pick me up tonight."

"Do you mean Rick?" Lana asked, her mouth feeling like it was suddenly filled with cotton balls.

Mrs. Schultz finished stacking the plates, clucking with satisfaction. "Yes, that's his name. Rick," she confirmed, shuddering. "Horrible child, reprehensible teenager, and I cannot even imagine what sort of man he has since grown into. Samantha never told me why, but I knew she didn't like to see him."

It suddenly registered with Lana that she could hear the ticking of the grandfather clock…and nothing else. The house was silent. She spun around, not seeing Gray anywhere, and a sick feeling of horror rose inside of her, but she forced herself to be reasonable.

"I wonder where Gray got off to," she remarked.

Mrs. Schultz had started wiping down the counters with quick efficiency, but she answered immediately. "Oh, I think I saw him headed to see what gifts I brought him in the bags that are still on the front steps." Her smile was indulgent. "He's such a sweet little boy."

Without stopping to explain, Lana sprinted to the front door. She noted absently that it wasn't latched, but of course, Mrs. Schultz had known that they would be coming back for the other bags, and it wasn't as if Lana had explained that they were under some unknown threat. Lana berated herself mercilessly as she flung the door open, hoping against hope that she'd find the little boy out there, safe and sound, or even halfway across the lawn, even though he knew very well he wasn't allowed out on the grounds by himself. Instead, she found that one of the suitcases was open, with one still-wrapped gift peeking out, but there was no sign whatsoever of Gray.

She ran down the steps, shouting his name, but even as she did so, she could feel it. He was gone. Something very bad had happened, and Sam's baby — the child who she had already come to love as fiercely as if he'd been her nephew or son all along — was missing.

Lana's mind flashed white for a second, almost as if she'd been shocked by electricity, and she felt all-consuming panic rise, along with bile, from deep in her gut up to her throat, but she determinedly swallowed it down, along with a lump that might have been a sob. Gray needed her to be calm...logical. There were security cameras and alarms everywhere, an ex-military team nearby. Mac...her mind seized on his image, and she wanted nothing more than to talk to Mac.

She pulled out her phone and pressed the keys to connect to Mac at the same time as she ran back and hit the flashing red panic button on the front door security alarm.

"Hey, there, darlin'," came Mac's easy drawl when he picked up, and he sounded pleased. "I've got good news... We finally traced the inheritance trail to some distant relative of Sam's, Broderick something."

She must have made some animal cry of distress because she heard Mac talking again on the other end of the line.

"Oh, God, Lana, are you there? What's wrong?" He sounded concerned and also like he might be running.

"I think Gray's gone," she blurted, trying to keep the hysterical note out of her voice, but failing. "Mrs. Schultz came back early, and he went out to the front steps, but he's not here and I think someone took him. I'm checking the house now to be sure he isn't hiding somewhere, but...I just... It sounds crazy, but I know it."

"Okay, honey. Is one of the guys there with you? Someone should have come when Mrs. Schultz arrived." Mac's voice was reassuringly calm and steady.

"No...nobody's here. I just pushed the panic button, too. It's just me and Mrs. Schultz and maybe some strange ride-share driver. Mrs. Schultz commented that the driver she had looked like Rick..." she trailed off, her mind racing furiously, even as she rushed from room to room inside the house. At the direction of her thoughts, her blood turned to ice in her veins.

"Wh-what did you say the name of the relative was? Broderick *what*?" she asked faintly, and she heard Mac curse on the other end of the line as he realized what she might be thinking.

"Here it is," Mac said, and she heard paper rustling. "Broderick Simpson," he confirmed, and it felt the bottom fell out of Lana stomach.

"*Rick* Simpson... Rick Simpson is Sam's distant relative." His name echoed in her head like a curse…like a nightmare that she'd never wake up from, coming to haunt her from the distant past. She staggered, holding herself up against the wall.

"Lana? Lana?" She could tell by his tone that Mac had said her name multiple times. "Sugar, say something or just make a noise so I know you're still there," Mac ordered.

"I'm here," she answered faintly, shaking her head to clear it. "I'm here."

"I'll be there in five minutes, and I'm gonna stay on the phone with you the whole time, but honey…I just got a message from Gun that the guy he had watching your feeds from close-by was found unconscious. They think he was drugged. Someone else will be coming, but…we have to find this guy fast."

"Yes, fast," she echoed, not clear on what he was getting at. She'd resumed her search of the house and was a bit out of breath.

"Gun's team is gonna do whatever they can, but, darlin', there are only so many of them, and they don't have many underground research resources. When time is of the essence, that kind of manpower and intel can usually be bought, though, for the right price and with the right contacts." Now, she understood. She knew what he was going to say before he finished.

"The kind of contacts my brothers and grandfather have," she finished. She considered it for a millisecond, the old resistance to asking her family for help, but really, it was just a silly holdover from a past that didn't matter at all in the face of danger to Gray.

"Call them… Call my family, the police, *everyone*. I don't care what it takes or costs." Her breath hitched on a sob as she pictured Gray, so small and sad, slow to warm up to strangers, being terrified and terrorized…or worse, maybe being hurt. She had to force her mind away from that possibility or she wouldn't be able to function, and Gray needed her now more than ever. "I will give or do *anything* to get him back," she finished, and it was a vow. She swiped furiously at the tears that leaked from the corners of her eyes.

"We *will* find him." Mac's voice was steely, and all traces of the charming Southern gentleman were gone. "And I will bring him back to you," he promised, and she prayed that he was right.

Chapter Seventeen

The next hour was quite possibly the worst and most chaotic of Mac's life—which, given his injury, was saying something—but he would have gone through his entire hospital stay and recovery again, if only to have Gray home safely. His ribcage felt too small for his heart and lungs when he thought of the small, red-headed preschooler who'd come to mean so much to him in a short time and who'd brought untold joy to the other adults in his life. Even now, Mrs. Schultz was still nearly inconsolable, having almost fainted when she realized the unwitting role she'd played in his abduction.

Their only comfort was that everyone agreed that Rick was extremely unlikely to want to kill Gray and that he'd had plenty of opportunities to do so before when he'd been terrorizing Lana and Gray. It was much more advantageous for Rick if he could somehow get Lana to relinquish her guardianship of Gray, allowing Rick to take over administration of the family trust, since no potential successor to Lana had yet been named by the trustees. Still, that might not stop Rick from hurting the little boy.

They'd confirmed from security footage that Gray had indeed been abducted, right from the front steps, only a matter of a couple of dozen feet from Lana and Mrs. Schultz, in broad daylight. Rick Simpson was a bold bastard. Mac would give him that.

Luckily, they'd figured out what Gun's crew-member had been drugged with and had been able to safely counteract it. Unfortunately, the man wasn't able to tell them anything other than that someone had snuck into his van and injected him with something. He was a tall, tough guy, but he'd still been shaken up…and they all realized that they were lucky Rick hadn't intended to do more harm.

Lana had spoken with Fitz and Clara first, catching them in spite of the generally bad cell reception because they'd been at their small cabin. The pair had immediately called one of the police officers who they'd gotten know very well over the course of the investigation surrounding the actions of Clara's ex. Mac thought that it probably owed more to the Fitzhugh name than the man himself, but Detective Bergsen had been happy to assist, and when he'd arrived a short while ago, he'd seemed just as thorough and competent as Fitz and Clara had indicated.

Lana was just finishing a second videocall with them now from the family room, and Mac had only gotten up to grab her something cool to drink. When he returned, Fitz was talking.

"…don't understand why you didn't tell us sooner what was going on." Fitz didn't sound angry so much as hurt.

Clara was sitting next to him on the screen, and she bounced baby Hope as they spoke. "You seemed relatively calm the last time I visited, with you and Gray both adjusting," Clara said.

Lana sighed, gratefully taking and sipping the ice water he handed her. "It didn't feel like anything was really wrong at first, then things got strange after you guys left on your trip, but...I didn't have any evidence."

"You had evidence enough to call MacKenzie," Fitz returned, glowering, and Mac understood that he wasn't going to be forgiven anytime soon by his friend.

"Look," Lana interjected, sounding and looking suddenly exhausted. "That isn't all of it. I didn't want to call you, Drew or Granda because I didn't want you to think of me as the same spoiled, shallow kid that I was—the one you had no respect for, and deservedly so. I've changed, but coming off as a crazy society princess who panics at shadows is not the way to help you or anyone else understand that."

Fitz frowned so hard that his forehead creased. "Lana, I know you're not the same kid you were when I left. God knows, I am definitely not the same arrogant SOB I was well on my way to becoming back then. I wouldn't think that... I know we're still catching up in some ways, but I see the woman you've become, and I'm in awe of you."

Clara reached for and squeezed Fitz's hand in a silent show of support.

Mac was shocked that Lana had spoken up, but even more so when another voice sounded from behind them, making Lana and him turn in their seats.

"Is that how I treat you, Lana?" Drew asked, obviously having just arrived and looking more rumpled than Mac could ever recall seeing him before. In fact, Mac would go so far as to call his appearance disheveled.

"What are you doing here, Drew?" Lana asked warily. "I thought you were in Munich for a few more days."

A hint of a wry smile touched Drew's lips, and the expression made Mac see more of a resemblance between him, Fitz, and Lana.

"Well, my sister's companion...boyfriend... whatever you are..." he motioned at Mac, and Mac braced himself for an insult. "*Mac* made some remarks that, ah, cut close to the bone, and I realized that I might have been, er, well, treating Lana like an ass over some ancient history — I mean I'm the ass in this scenario, not Lana — so I tried to call to apologize, and they wouldn't take my calls, so I arranged an earlier flight."

Fitz, Lana and Clara all wore equally shocked expressions, and Mac thought that his face probably mirrored theirs.

Lana was the first to speak. "You...*you, Drew* Fitzhugh, left a conference days before it ended and caught an earlier flight, because you wanted to apologize to me, *Lana* Fitzhugh?" she said incredulously.

Drew frowned at her as if she had grown an extra eyebrow. "I know you're very overwrought, which is why I'm glad I was already on my way, but it isn't like you to be so confused, Lana. Have I really never apologized to you?"

Lana shut her mouth with a snap. "In a word, no. No, you haven't."

Drew looked uncomfortable, but he drew himself up to his full height, which was just a little shorter than

Mac's six feet and two inches. "Well, then, I should have. I'm sorry for the way I've been treating you, as if I'm incapable of listening to or respecting you. I'm not...very good at showing emotions or admitting when I'm wrong, but I'm trying to be better."

Lana stood and crossed the room to her brother, putting her arms around him. Drew looked discomfited but put his arms around her as well to return her hug. Now it made sense to Mac why he hadn't been able to get through to Drew earlier, and he was happy for Lana. She'd said she didn't want it to matter, but the challenges with her family had obviously left an indelible mark on her. This unexpected gesture could go a significant distance in the family building a new, better relationship. It appeared Drew wasn't finished yet, though, when he spoke again.

"Regarding Gray's abduction, I've been calling everyone, putting the word out, but I haven't had any credible follow-ups yet. With the amount of money that I'm hinting we're offering, I'd be surprised if I don't get some calls within the next half-hour or so." Drew was so matter-of-fact about helping locate Gray that it would have been easy to overlook the magnitude of what he was doing, what he was committing.

"Thank you," Lana whispered to him, sounding tearful, and before Mac realized it, he was up and out of his seat as well, crossing the room to shake Drew's hand.

"Thank you from me, too," he added, his voice hoarse with suppressed emotion. Fitz, Lana and Mac's combined connections couldn't compare to those of Drew Fitzhugh, known worldwide to be utterly ruthless in business—particularly about his family—

and wealthy beyond belief, with nearly unlimited resources. For the first time since Lana had called to tell him Gray had been taken, Mac felt a true flicker of hope in his gut.

When the front door flew open again with a ringing bang, Mac was almost afraid to look past Lana's brother to see what new person had now entered. If he were a betting man, Pat Fitzhugh wouldn't have been even on his top five list, but there the elder Fitzhugh was, looking thinner and frailer than ever, and sitting in a wheelchair, pushed by Roger. Pat's face, though, held an expression of grim determination.

"Granda?" Drew and Lana asked simultaneously, and Mac heard an echo of the question from the laptop that he'd forgotten they'd left in the other room, with Fitz and Clara still on the videocall.

"We're here to go get the little laddie," Pat announced in a firm voice that echoed in the large space. The police had just left, save one younger officer who was stationed outside, but Gun and a couple of his guys remained in the kitchen, along with Mrs. Schultz, and of course Drew, Lana and Mac. There was a collective hush as everyone gaped at Pat.

Pat raised his eyebrows disdainfully. "I'm not here to go m'self. I'm not that foolish…or rather, the spirit is willing, but I know when my body is and isn't, and today we're havin' an off day. However, Roger has used his connections to find out some very interesting information."

Lana had mentioned just the day before that she'd always wondered if Roger had secretly come from — or might still be a part of — a dark ops organization, like the CIA or something else, and Mac had confessed that he'd always gotten a deep ops vibe from Roger, too, who was crazy fit for a man his age. He also seemed to know everything about everyone, always, and Lana had confirmed that he'd always been that way.

Roger stepped forward, looking as proper and unassuming as always. "I have a friend who I believe has successfully convinced one of Mr. Simpson's, *erm*, associates to provide us his last known address. I cannot divulge from whence this information has come." He looked in turn at everyone in the room, and Mac understood the unspoken message. This was unofficial and needed to remain secret. Everyone nodded, even Mrs. Schultz.

"Due to this tip's provenance, I cannot allow the police to be involved...at least not until we know what we're going to find. Therefore, I would ask that we form two groups. One will be responsible for...shall we say, redirecting the police? Only temporarily, mind you."

"I volunteer to lead that group," Pat interjected gleefully, steepling his hands.

"The other, which I volunteer to lead—in fact, I insist—will be a covert infiltration of the address, where we will locate and remove the young Master Erasmus at all costs. I do not state this lightly... I will be removing him at *any* cost."

Mac had had seen his share of brothers, Navy and otherwise, headed into the most dangerous missions, and he recognized the same dark determination on Roger's face as he'd seen on those men's and women's faces...and as he thought might be on his own face now.

"I volunteer for team two," he said, stepping forward.

His heart swelled with equal parts pride and terror as he heard Lana's voice ring out. "So do I. In fact, I insist."

* * * *

The last known address for Rick Simpson was a small mechanic's shop in an out-of-the way, nearly abandoned industrial neighborhood on the outskirts of Minneapolis. At least to Lana's eyes, the architecture was colorless and grim, and everyone — the very few people — they'd passed had seemed just as beaten down as the buildings. Since they'd left, loading up into a high-tech van that Roger had somehow gotten ahold of for the day, her grandfather's companion had proven to the small group of Mac, Gun, Lana and both of the other guys from Gun's team, Carlson and Jones, in countless ways that he was intimately familiar with both intrigue and leadership. They'd parked several blocks from the final address, and split into three separate sub-groups, each with a different goal.

Carlson and Jones were going to be the distraction. Neither of them had been onsite regularly at Gray's house, so they were the most logical choice. Roger and Gun were going to sneak into the building and incapacitate everyone they came across. Since they didn't have any idea of the scale or number of men they might find, this was significantly riskier, but both Gun and Roger seemed more than willing. Lana and Mac made up the final sub-group, and their sole job was to locate and secure Gray. Since he knew both of them, this was also the only logical choice. In fact, Lana was now certain that if he hadn't wanted to be sure that Gray recognized his rescuers, Roger would have happily tied her to a chair in some super-secret soundproof basement dungeon and left her behind entirely.

Actually, now that she was seeing Roger in an entirely new light, she wondered if her own family home might possess a super-secret soundproof basement dungeon. She stored away the idea to mention to Mac later. Maybe he'd go exploring with her.

Recalling herself to the task at hand, she turned to Mac silently, watching the graceful way he moved, incredibly stealthy in spite of the change in his gait forced by his prosthesis. All six of them had agreed not to speak for the duration of the mission, and unfortunately, while the other men easily used hand signals, she had just had to noiselessly mouth the two things she'd needed to say to Mac so far.

The back of the shop loomed in front of them, surrounded by a tall silver chain-link fence, which was covered all over with panels of corrugated plastic sheeting. It was topped with a full complement of barbed wire, but the whole effect of tight security was spoiled by the fact that there were numerous gaps in the fencing, including one at the gate that looked more than wide enough for Mac and her to slip through. Her heart pounded with a mix of adrenaline and fear, but underneath it, hope swelled. She couldn't wait for the moment when she could hold Gray in her arms again, rock him to sleep, cuddle him next to her and never let him go. She didn't even care what happened to Rick at this point...if only they could find Gray safe and sound.

She forced herself to take three deep breaths, letting them out slowly, and squared her shoulders. *I never would have imagined that my yoga breathing could come in so darn handy on dangerous missions*, she mused. *Maybe I'll get to use some Zumba moves inside*, she thought, a little wildly. When they had reached the gate, Mac looked her questioningly, making an 'okay' symbol with his fingers and raising one eyebrow.

She flashed him a smile—which she hoped was a reassuring one—and a thumbs-up, and he slipped in through the gap first. They'd talked about the order of entry ahead of time, with Mac insisting that he would go first so he'd be the target if they found anything unexpected. She shivered now as she waited for the longest count of ten of her life, praying that she wouldn't hear anything bad from the other side of the fence. When she'd finished counting, she slipped through the gap, nearly weak with relief when she saw Mac there waiting for her, and she bent over to make herself lower to the ground. They made their way around several burned-looking shells of cars before they got to the back of the building, which had one garage door that appeared stuck half-open.

"Nobody's ever gonna find us here, and Lana Fitzhugh is too stupid to even try to hire the right kind of people to try to take us on. It's an easy job, and nobody's gonna hurt the kid, so no need to get squeamish on that front."

Lana's gut clenched as she recognized the voice she hadn't heard in years outside of her nightmares. *Rick Simpson*. After all this time, he was still talking crap about her, too. They couldn't see him, but it sounded like he was on the phone, a guess that was confirmed when she heard the distinctive, tinny version of a voice on the other end of a connection.

"It's your loss, man. Because we've been friends for a long time, I was just trying to give you a chance to get in on the ground floor. I'll be able to do whatever I want soon, as long as that bitch Lana resigns as guardian for Grayson and lead trustee before someone else can be appointed by the estate."

Lana inwardly cheered at hearing the proof that what Mac and Gun had suspected was accurate and was a clear motive for Rick. She had full confidence that Roger was recording, as he'd planned, and would ensure that everyone received proof of what Rick had attempted to do.

"Oh, hey, fine. I gotta go anyway. Looks like there are some guys here who are either ridiculously confused or idiots. Hopefully both...just how I like 'em."

They heard Rick shuffle to the front of the building, and Lana put her hand on Mac's arm, pointing toward what must have once been the office area of the shop. He nodded his understanding, and they headed there with painful slowness, stopping to look around every few feet. Lana's heart initially fell when they got to the door and found it closed, but then soared again as she heard a faint noise from within. She caught Mac's gaze, and his was practically crackling with intensity as he silently gestured to himself, clearly indicating he would take the lead.

He eased open the door with more patience than she thought she'd ever possessed in her entire life while she waited on edge, poised to one side, ready to either escape if the office's occupant turned out to be an accomplice, or run inside if — as she hoped and prayed — they found Gray there. As the door slowly swung open on blessedly silent hinges and she saw Gray's solemn little face, smudged by something dark that might be either dirt or bruises, her knees went so weak that she feared for a moment she might collapse, but Mac was right there beside her, steadying her, ready to hold her up.

Just as she held a finger to her lips to tell Gray to stay silent, she heard Roger's distinctive voice ring out. "The building and surrounding area is all clear, and we have Simpson and his accomplice in custody with police *en route*. Have we located the child?"

She crouched down and held out her arms, and with a joyful cry, Gray barreled into her arms so fast that he knocked her over so that she sat on the cold concrete floor hugging him like she never wanted to let him go.

"Affirmative," Mac's steady voice called out the response. "We've located and secured him, and he's currently being hugged by Lana."

Chapter Eighteen

Lana sat with Gray and Mac in the van, now parked out front of the dingy mechanic's shop, as Roger, Gun, Carlson and Jones all fielded questions from the police, who had arrived a short time earlier. Lana had seen the naked skepticism in Detective Bergsen's expression when Roger had told him that they'd all been driving around the city and just happened to spot something suspicious at this particular mechanic shop, which had led to them finding Gray. It was patently ridiculous, and Lana couldn't believe how smoothly Roger delivered the untruth. Still, maybe mollified by the Fitzhugh name or maybe more by the fact that they had found Gray safe and sound, the detective seemed to be letting it slide.

The number of police officers who had arrived, along with the general chaos of the scene, had started to be overwhelming for Gray, so Mac had guided them back to the van. He didn't seem to be able to stop touching either Lana or Gray — subtle touches, like on her hair or arm — and Lana understood, since she felt the need to continue to brush her fingers over Gray's head, just to reassure herself that he was really all right. They sat on a bench seat together, with Lana so close to Mac that she was nearly on top of him, and with Gray in turn on her lap, still clutched tightly in her arms.

"Wanna go home," Gray said, turning his face into her chest so his voice was muffled.

Lana could sympathize. She wanted nothing more than to go back to the house and lock themselves up tightly for the next week or so…maybe a month. "I know, baby. We just have to stay while everyone finishes up here, but we'll go home as soon as we can."

Mac was rubbing her back soothingly — she hadn't been sure he was even aware he was doing it — and now he squeezed her shoulder reassuringly.

"They're taking Rick?" Gray asked.

Lana tensed. Other than reassuring Gray and asking whether he was all right, she hadn't wanted to push him for information and also hadn't wanted to inadvertently bring any bad memories back to the little boy, who had seemed content to be silent as she held him.

"They're taking him," she confirmed in a careful tone.

Gray nodded. "That's okay. He's not nice. He lied to me and locked me in a smelly room." He burrowed more snugly against her. "I wanted you and Mac to come, and you did," he said, his tone growing tired.

Lana's vision was blurry with tears as she exchanged a look with Mac, who put his arm fully around her so that he was hugging both her and Gray. She understood what he didn't say out loud. She felt it, too. When the medic — closely supervised by Mac — had wiped at the smudge on Gray's face and it had turned out to be dirt after all, she'd felt a sort of bone-deep relief. Now, hearing this apparent confirmation from Gray that he hadn't been hurt—even though she was certain that it had been horrible to be taken and locked in a strange room—brought an additional layer of indescribable gratitude. In Gray's mind, he'd been uncomfortable and wanted to leave, and Lana and Mac had come to get him.

She tried not to squeeze him too tightly, although it was difficult. "Of course," she whispered. "We love you, baby."

"Love you, too," Gray murmured sleepily, and she realized that it must be around his naptime. *How is it possible that so much has happened in the space of only a few hours?* The time, along with the stress of the day's events, must have completely tired him out.

The sound of his breathing, deep and even with the slightest hint of a snore, filled the van, and it was clear he'd dozed off. Lana couldn't help but press another kiss to the top of Gray's head, inhaling the familiar scent of his baby shampoo.

"Mac, I was so scared," she admitted in a whisper.

"Me too, darlin'...*God*, me, too," he answered, his voice raw with emotion. "You didn't look scared, though. You looked like a freakin' Amazon." He pulled her to him almost impossibly closer, squeezing her so she thought her ribs might be bruised, but she didn't care. "I'm so goddamn thankful." His voice was thick...with tears?

A mix of emotions swelled within Lana. "I'm sorry for the way I acted," she blurted out before she could second-guess herself.

"What?" Mac's tone was surprised. "You were amazin', sugar, and I am in awe."

Lana shifted slightly so she could turn to him more fully. His face was half in shadow, but half illuminated by the afternoon sunlight that filtered in through the tinted van windows, making his one eye look a startling, vibrant green. Where the sun hit it, his hair — and even his eyebrow — looked almost like gold leaf.

"You were the brave one, Mac... God, when you slipped through the fence without a second's hesitation, knowing you could be walking right into danger or even a trap." She felt her eyes sting again. "I was terrified for you."

His expression grew soft, but she thought she saw some deeper feeling in his eyes as well.

"I was apologizing for earlier, though. This morning," she clarified.

Mac drew his eyebrows together, and she noticed again how ridiculously long his eyelashes were. How could a man have such beautiful eyelashes but still look so decidedly masculine? Rugged, even?

"Darlin', I told you I understood. There's no need to apologize," he answered.

"No," she shook her head. "There is. I promised myself I'd tell you this as soon as I could." She raised her chin, steadying herself. If she could be part of a potentially dangerous covert rescue mission, she could find the courage to be honest with Mac about her feelings. "I thought about it after you left, and I haven't been fair to you. I've let my past color my feelings so deeply that I don't even realize it, but Mac, I care about you, too. I want a future with you. I'm so sorry I pushed you away. I think I was just so happy that it scared me. Do you...? Can we keep trying? If you're willing?"

"Lana, honey, there is nothin' I would like better than a future with you, forever. I can — and will — give you any time and space that you need, only I hope that we can get to wherever we're goin' together, with you in my bed every night and you so well-loved you glow with satisfaction. I want you to know — to truly feel it — that it's what you deserve. Nothing less."

Now, Lana didn't even try to hold in the tears that filled her eyes and ran down cheeks.

"Mac...you're so..." She struggled to think of the right words, words that would fully encompass how much she cared for him. "You're everything," she settled on. "You're my everything...handsome, sexy, funny, brilliant, patient, kind, loyal... How could I not fall in love with you?"

He had been looking alarmed at the sudden onset of her tears, but as she spoke, his expression gentled. "Did you...? Darlin', did you just say that you love me?" he asked, the words coming out slightly strangled.

"So much, Mac," she confirmed in a husky voice.

He closed his eyes, and when he opened them, his face was joyful. "I love you, too, Lana. I think I have for a long while, but I didn't want to spook you. You're my everythin' as well, darlin' — everythin' and more, like the other half of me." He tightened his arm around her again and leaned down to kiss her. He teased her with his lips and tongue, and she responded with passion, longing to wrap her arms around him — heck, to wrap her legs around him — but she held herself back, afraid of waking up Gray.

When they pulled apart, they were both breathing hard.

"Ah, sugar, you have no idea how badly I wish we were alone at home right now," he breathed, sounding as frustrated as she felt.

"I bet I do," she returned in a sassy tone.

His bark of laughter was so loud that it echoed in the small space, but Gray didn't move a muscle, and his breathing remained steady.

"I love it when you get feisty," Mac said, and his eyes held a touch of wickedness.

Lana snorted, and the sound was not ladylike in the least. Her mother would have been horrified. "You're in luck, then, because I tend to get feisty pretty regularly," she admitted ruefully. A hint of some of the old doubts began to creep in. "Are you sure about this? I'm not always easy — pretty far from perfect, in fact."

Mac squeezed her shoulder again. "I'm sure," he said firmly, and she couldn't doubt that he meant it. "And, Lana, you don't have to be perfect, not for me or anyone else. All you have to be is yourself, because you're wonderful. Any time you forget, I'll be right here to remind you."

Her heart melted at his earnest tone, and the naked emotion she read in his eyes. "You're wonderful, too," she whispered.

Mac raised one eyebrow. "Well, now, I think I liked your other list better," he teased. "What did you call me? Handsome, funny, brilliant? Did you mention sexy?" He pressed another kiss to her lips. "Because that is a very important quality of mine. I am wildly sexy."

She pretended to consider the question seriously. "I thought I mentioned it, but maybe I forgot."

"I think you need a thorough reminder, then." His voice was so gravelly as he spoke low, near her ear, that she shivered. "As soon as we get home, darlin'."

Epilogue

"How long do we have?" Mac asked in a growly voice as he tackled her to the bed as soon as she entered the room.

"Mm-m," Lana moaned at the feeling of the kisses he was pressing down her neck. "Clara said she and Fitz would keep Gray for at least two hours."

"Good. I can do a lot with two hours," Mac answered, running one hand up the outside of her thigh to push up the mid-length skirt she wore while stroking her hair with his other hand.

Lana gave herself over to the sensation of his touch, but then a horrible thought occurred to her, making her suddenly go still. Clara had been really specific when she'd said how long they would be gone. "Wait! Do you think they know what we're doing?"

"Oh yeah." Mac's voice was muffled against her neck, and she thought that he was likely headed toward her breasts. The man couldn't seem to get enough of her nipples—which worked out perfectly, since she couldn't get enough of his attention to them. "They're a couple who has a baby. Clara *definitely* knows what we're doing," he confirmed.

Lana squeaked with alarm and tried to push him off her. "Oh my God! That's...terrible!"

"Terrible," Mac agreed, pushing down the wide neck of her shirt along with the cups of her bra so that he could get to her nipples, which instantly hardened in the cool air, practically begging for his touch.

"It's...scandalous," Lana continued, but the word came out as more of a sigh of pleasure as Mac closed his lips around one peak.

"Mm-hmm." He made a sound of assent against the mound of her breast, and the vibration made her quiver.

"But I guess it would"—Lana broke off with a gasp as Mac slid his hand into her panties and cupped her mound, making her core go hot and liquid—"would be rude to ask them to come home now. We wouldn't want to offend them."

Mac's expression was both wicked and amused as he lifted his head to look at her. "We wouldn't want to be rude," he agreed, circling his finger around her bundle of nerves with exquisite gentleness, just the way she liked best, and making her moan and clutch at him. She was so distracted by what he was doing that she almost didn't hear his next words. "After all, we'll probably want to ask them to be the best man and maid of honor at our wedding."

When the words registered, she froze and looked up at him in wonder. "What did you just say?"

Mac's green eyes were filled with love, and his lips looked soft and kissable as the corners of his mouth curved into a crooked smile. "I might have spoken a little out of turn — *again* — but I want us to get married. I'm hopin' — *really* hopin' — you'll agree to be my wife, Lana."

A wave incandescent happiness rose inside of her, filling her to the brim until there wasn't room for anything else. "Yes," she breathed. "Yes...yes, yes, *yes!*"

"Was that a yes?" Mac asked teasingly. "You were a little unclear."

She swatted at his shoulder playfully, and the movement made her realize that, while he'd stopped stroking her, he still had his hand in her underwear and her breasts were bare between them.

"You're lucky I agreed," she answered. "For the record, Lieutenant Commander MacKenzie, it might be considered bad form to propose to a girl right in the middle of groping her," she scolded him, but without any real heat.

"Hm, fair point, future-Mrs.-MacKenzie. However, this way I am in a unique strategic position to immediately make that girl forget any irregularities in the method of my proposal, aren't I?" he answered, winking shamelessly before he resumed his caresses of her core.

Lana exhaled on a whimper of pure pleasure. Mac had shown her so many ways they could touch and love each other, but he was constantly still surprising her. "Okay, I'm willing to let you make it up to me," she answered breathlessly.

"Very generous of you." Mac's voice was laden with suppressed laughter.

"You'd better get going," she urged. "You only have two hours."

His rich chuckle filled her with joy.

Want to see more from this author? Here's a taster for you to enjoy!

Secret Santa:
Her Special Ops Santa
Aurora Russell

Coming December 2022

Excerpt

T.J.'s nose itched. It had, in fact, been itching like hell for over an hour, but he wouldn't scratch it. His cover was too damn uncertain, and he couldn't risk any movement until he got the intel he was waiting for. Instead, he deliberately relaxed each muscle in his body one by one, starting from the small muscles of his toes and going all the way up to his face and scalp, using incremental movements. After so long in one position, he needed to regularly ensure that his body remained limber, ready for action on a millisecond's notice.

I'm getting too old for this shit, he thought dryly, feeling the ache of every single old injury to his thirty-eight-year-old body. *Maybe I'll put in that retirement paperwork after this mission.* He tested out the idea in his mind and found that he didn't hate it. Then again, what on God's green Earth else would someone like him do? He figured he would probably be a lifer.

A couple of hours before dawn that morning, as his elite unit of Marines had been gearing up to jump off the side of their small ship to swim to their precarious positions, Bulldog had joked that they were getting to be dinosaurs in Force Recon years. T.J. had laughed it off—and Bulldog had always been easy to laugh with, lightening the mood of every mission since they'd gone through special forces training together with the rest of his unit—but now he wondered if his friend and teammate didn't have a point.

T.J. lay prone under scant cover in a shallow depression he'd hastily dug into the hard, rocky ground, coated in dried mud. It had been the only spot close enough to surveille his assigned section of the back wall of the U.S. Embassy that had become ground zero for the current terrorist uprising in the impoverished Middle Eastern country that had heretofore been relatively peaceful. Usually, he reveled in the thrill of the mission, the ever-present danger. He loved the feeling that came over him, the confidence that he would prevail over whatever awaited, that made him feel twice as alive. Today, though, he just felt itchy.

Without conscious thought—and after so many missions, it had become second nature, just another part of him, like breathing or blinking—he constantly scanned the landscape around him as well as the walls that surrounded the embassy. The heat of the afternoon bled into the slow cool-down that signaled the start of the dusk. In spite of the occasional loud noises from within, everything remained quiet from his position until he saw it…then again. *Yes*, there was the slightest movement behind the faint outline of a door built into the light, stone walls, coated with the dust that blew everywhere. T.J. continued to hold still, but he felt an echo of that familiar zing of excitement in his stomach. *This* was what he'd been waiting for.

Two figures, dressed in black paramilitary uniforms and toting what looked like older-model AK-47s, crept stealthily from the door. Actually, they were pretty good at being unobtrusive. In the waning light, with the lengthening shadows, someone else might have missed them. Not T.J., of course, but someone who hadn't had his training and mission experience. Not for the first time, he was struck by how painfully young the militants looked—like kids playing dress-up in uniforms. Armed kids, filled with rage, but with baby fat still in their cheeks. He didn't make the mistake of underestimating them, though. He'd seen that kind of mistake cost lives.

Oblivious to their audience, the two young men walked closer to him, and he had a moment's flare of unease that they might actually step on him, but they paused a few feet away. His ears practically twitched, and he couldn't believe his good goddamn luck when they started to speak. Their voices were low, but he was so close it wasn't even much of a strain to hear them. They spoke in the local dialect of Arabic, but he was passably fluent in several, including that one. It was one of the reasons he'd been chosen for this mission—why his whole team had.

"The Americans probably think we're too stupid to guard this door." The first young man's voice dripped with disdain, and he switched his weapon from one shoulder to the other, puffing up his skinny chest.

"It's not on any of the plans...and it is nearly impossible to see from the outside if you don't know where it is already. We wouldn't have found it if there weren't a traitor loyal to our cause."

T.J.'s mind raced. It was confirmation of what they'd suspected, and it wasn't good...but it certainly explained why it had seemed like the insurgents anticipated every move before the guards inside the embassy could make them.

The second speaker, who looked slightly older, grew thoughtful before he spoke again. "In fact, I think we should use it. We can set a trap for whatever rescuers the Americans think to send. We'll make it seem as though we never discovered the passageway out...leaving it look unguarded. But we'll have four or five men inside waiting to pick them off as they enter — the hallway is too narrow for more. It'll be a squeeze for five."

"We don't need five. Four good, strong soldiers and the will of Allah will make us victorious." In spite of the lengthening shadows, T.J. could see the light of fanaticism burning bright and feverish in the younger man's eyes.

"We may need only four, but five will guarantee that we bring death to all of them." The second man's smile was cold but then widened into something almost feral. "In fact, I love knowing that they will be so close to the survivors who barricaded themselves in the safe room, but we'll slaughter them like goats before they can reach the doors."

T.J. remained perfectly still as the two young terrorists stalked back toward the entrance, his thoughts chaotic. *Fuck.* They *had* hoped the passageway had remained secret so his team could use it to access the embassy. Still, it was better that he'd overheard their plans so they could anticipate and work around the ambush...and in fact, the info that there were survivors in the safe room was an added bonus. This situation was still royally FUBAR — fucked up beyond all recognition—but he and his team were elite operatives who only got sent in when everything was going to shit...or had already gone there.

As he was running potential scenarios in his mind, intending to remain perfectly still until full dark so he could make his way back to the rendezvous point and deliver his report, he heard the barest disturbance, nearly lost to the wind. It sounded almost like a heavy animal but...*not*. It took him a moment to figure out where it was coming from, and when he did, he swore under his breath.

What the ever-loving fuck is she doing?

The figure he saw emerging from the rocky outcroppings that led toward one of the poorer residential neighborhoods was unmistakably feminine, with soft curves and graceful movements. It was impossible to tell if she were American or some other nationality, but she didn't look like a local. Some of her clothes had dark brown stains, although if it were blood, it likely wasn't all hers if she'd been able to walk such a good distance, and she was clutching something to her chest. He silently willed her to stop, since her current path could possibly take her directly into the line of fire of the two bloodthirsty young terrorists he'd just eavesdropped on, but she persisted, and he had to admire her bravery...along with her beauty.

Holy hell, she looked sweet...like every dream he'd thought he'd long ago given up on, but what was a woman like her doing out here in the dry landscape of the back door to hell? And during a highly publicized terrorist uprising, no less? It was killing him to remain still. They were getting more cover by the second from the setting sun, so if she only paused for a minute or two, he'd be able to run to help her.

He couldn't help but twitch in spite of all his training and practice when he realized that what she held was a distinctive blue passport with what appeared to be the familiar glinting golden eagle. *Well, shit.* She was American. When the orange-and-red glow of the dying sunset hit her face and showed traces of tears down her cheeks, he tensed, and something twisted in his chest at the idea of her being hurt. *Fuck it.* He wasn't going to wait until full sunset when she needed him now.

Rose Abbott had had an extremely crappy past thirty-six hours. First, they'd gotten the news at the clinic where she'd worked as a nurse for the past six months that a terrorist cell — one that had been growing in strength and violence — had somehow managed to take over the American embassy. That had been terrifying, especially because of how worried it made her for Alec. On top of it, she'd been forced to face the fact that her three fellow American aid workers weren't what she'd thought they were when a young patient of theirs, the sixteen-year-old wife of a much-older local businessman, had come in with clear signs of advanced labor and significant distress.

Rose tried to tell herself that she didn't blame Terry, Cal or Anne…and part of her didn't. It was some scary crap, suddenly not knowing if you could be a target anywhere you went, and she understood that they'd gone to flee the country as fast as they could. That had been her plan as well, before she'd seen Yemina…and the look of panic mixed with agony on the young girl's face. Yemina, and probably the baby as well, very likely would have died if she hadn't stayed there. The breech birth had been difficult, and she thanked God Yemina had arrived when she had, but then the hemorrhage afterward had been a full-on emergency. Thankfully,

Rose had stopped the bleeding and administered a blood transfusion, but it had been touch-and-go for a bit. She'd thanked the stars for every second of her grueling ER, trauma and OB nursing training. She'd only been able to leave when the local nurse Yemina's husband had managed to hire—probably mostly for the baby boy—had arrived to take over ongoing monitoring.

Rose took a deep breath, nearly choking on the dry dust that swirled around her. She, at least, had known about the back entrance to the embassy that Alec had sworn her to secrecy on. Her colleagues had had no such luxury. As she thought her brother's name, a squeeze of dread clenched her gut. Was he all right? Had he been injured or killed during the attack on the embassy? Or was he even now waiting for her in the safe room, worried sick?

A movement from off to her right made her freeze, and she squinted her eyes to try see better. Between the waning light and the haze created by the dust in the wind, she had trouble making anything out clearly. *Shoot.* She'd hoped to get to the back entrance before dark. In spite of the sometimes-scorching heat of the day, it got really cold very quickly out here at night. Her heart thudded nearly right out of her chest as an enormous figure emerged out of the dimness, and she would have screamed but he—and it was definitely a man—muffled any sound by putting one massive hand over her mouth. He wrapped his other arm around her waist and pulled her tightly against him, and her breath puffed out of her nose in short, panicked gasps.

She struggled against his hold, trying to bite his hand, to make herself heavy by going limp, then when that didn't work, by flailing like a wildcat in a snare, but the sound of his low voice near her ear stopped her.

"I'm so sorry to scare you, ma'am, but I had to stop you before you walked into the trap. I know you're American, and I'm a…friend."

His voice was deep and sensual, and his distinctly Southern accent so beautiful she could have cried. *Again.* Her hand tightened around the American passport that she still held. She'd gotten it out before heading to the embassy, thinking to display it if she needed to, but she realized she must have continued clutching it to herself like some sort of talisman until she'd forgotten it was even there.

Her brain told her to be wary. There was no reason the stranger couldn't be lying. He could be a mercenary, a human-trafficker, a traitor…any number of unsavory things. Even if her instincts told her that she could trust him, she needed to be cautious. She gave a minuscule nod of understanding that he seemed to feel against his hand or down his arm, and he grunted his acknowledgment.

"I'm goin' to take us back down to the ground, now, behind those rocks. If I take away my hand, will you promise not to make a sound?"

It was oddly intimate, him pressed so tightly against her that she could smell his sweat, the dirt on his skin and clothing and faint traces of his deodorant. His voice was a mere thread of a whisper in her ear. She gave her muffled assent and he slowly took his hand away from her mouth, so that she could suck in a deep—but silent—breath.

As promised, he tandem-walked them over to a nearby group of rocks, his movements shockingly fluid and graceful for such a big man. He eased them down to the ground with deliberation, until she was pressed to the rocky dirt, and he lay spread on top of her. *Covering me,* she realized. He was covering her from any gunfire, and he had been positioning his body even as they'd moved so that if shots were fired from the embassy walls, he'd be the one hit. Her heart clenched in her chest.

She took another deep breath, intending to ask him who, exactly, he was, but he stopped her with a gentle finger on her lips.

"No explanations...not now, not safe. We can move to a small cave soon, talk there."

She stiffened beneath his sizable bulk, her skin going icy with fear at the mention of a cave — a small, enclosed space for them to be alone...or maybe where accomplices waited. She'd been foolish to try him as far as she had. He was a stranger...more than that, he felt dangerous, menacing. If he were feline, and most men were housecats, he would be a tiger or jaguar. Her mind raced with plans to push him off her and escape.

His sigh was somehow nearly silent, but regretful.

"Hell...and now you're scared. How about if I give you a knife? Can we cut through the bullshit explanations and jump to you trustin' me? If they see us — catch us — we're both dead."

She turned her head and could only make out the profile of his face. His nose was very prominent, she thought absently, with a bit of a hook, and it looked like it had been broken before. *Not a charmer*, she mused, and it was oddly comforting.

"Give me the knife," she whispered, a mere breath of sound. She swore she felt him shudder behind her but thought she must have imagined it. As he shifted on top of her, presumably to take out the promised weapon, she felt something big and hard — and growing — press against the mounds of her ass, and she gave a small squeak of surprise before she could stifle it.

"Sorry," the soldier said, sounding chagrined. "You feel so fuckin' good. Can't help it. Just, uh, ignore it."

As if she could ignore something that felt that large...but he sounded so apologetic and embarrassed that she vowed to try to do as he'd asked. With a slight huff, he settled back over her, and pushed the hilt of a good-sized knife that she guessed would be well-maintained and well-used, into her free hand. She closed her grip around it and instantly felt more secure. First her father, then her brother, had trained her well in how to use a knife to defend herself. While the stranger might outweigh her and be able to overpower her, armed with his knife, she was confident she stood a good chance of doing serious enough damage to get away from him.

"Thank you," she whispered. She spoke so quietly that she worried he wouldn't hear her, but he must have had ears like a bat and gave a soft rumble of acknowledgment that she felt more than heard along her back.

In spite of the dangerous circumstance—in fact, maybe partly because of it—she felt curiously cherished and protected...safe. Weirdly, she felt the stirrings of possible attraction and arousal, which would be the height of foolishness. She ruthlessly quashed them and focused on reviewing the moves she would make if the stranger attacked her...although really, he hadn't had to give her his knife. He'd put himself at her mercy and, as he'd obviously hoped, it had helped her trust him.

"Feel better? Enough to let me take you to the cave?" His mouth was so close to her ear, she could feel his hot breath fan her hair and cheek. Goosebumps rose on her skin.

Am I willing to jump off the proverbial cliff with him and go to an unknown, secluded location? Rose squeezed her fingers around the hilt of the weapon, stroking her index finger up onto the side of the cool blade, and it grounded her. Still, she needed to remain logical. The knife could have been a calculated move to gain her trust and get her alone…but to what end? He already basically had her under his control. No…even thinking logically, he probably was what he seemed to be, some sort of dangerous, elite American security officer or special forces—yeah, special forces sounded right—and when she'd stumbled into his path, he'd done the honorable thing and saved her. In fact, he was probably risking his mission even now, and if she believed him about the trap, he was in much more danger with her than if he'd just let her walk into it.

"Your name?" she breathed.

He was silent and still for so long that she thought he wouldn't answer.

"T.J.," he finally responded, his voice terse for all that it was low.

"T.J.," she echoed. "I'll go with you, but if you try anything, you will bleed."

"Yes, ma'am," he whispered, and she thought maybe she detected admiration before he rose straight up like a silent wraith, displaying incredible strength, before pulling her to her feet and leading her into the inky black unknown of the night around them.

About the Author

Aurora is originally from the frozen tundra of the upper-Midwest (ok, not frozen all the time!) but now loves living in New England with her real-life hero/husband, two wonderfully silly sons, and one of the most extraordinary cats she has ever had the pleasure to meet. But she still goes back to the Midwest to visit, just never in January.

She doesn't remember a time that she didn't love to read, and has been writing stories since she learned how to hold a pencil. She has always liked the romantic scenes best in every book, story, and movie, so one day she decided to try her hand at writing her own romantic fiction, which changed her life in all the best ways.

Aurora loves to hear from readers. You can find her contact information, website details and author profile page at https://www.totallybound.com

Home of Erotic Romance

Sign up for our newsletter and find out about all our romance book releases, eBook sales and promotions, sneak peeks and FREE romance books!

www.ingramcontent.com/pod-product-compliance
Lightning Source LLC
Chambersburg PA
CBHW050736180626
46814CB00002B/780